"My son has bee.. ...., ...
seems to be able to find even the slightest trace of him."

"Before we get into that, I would like to know who you
are, sir?" I asked, interrupting him.

"Oh, I'm sorry. My name is Neil J. Cox."

"Well, Mr. Cox, finding people is the kind of work we
do, but I must tell you that this kind of case often ends up
unsolved. The older the case, the harder it is to solve. The
longer a case goes unsolved, the more difficult it becomes to
find clues that would help us find your son. Then there's the
problem of finding witnesses that are reliable. That makes it
almost impossible in older cases like what you are talking
about. Five years is a long time in a missing person case."

"I understand that, but I'm willing to pay whatever it
costs for you to find him, or at the very least, find out what
happened to my son."

"Sir, it is often not a matter of money. Assuming that
your son is alive; if he doesn't wish to be found, it becomes
almost impossible to find him."

"Mr. McCord, I have already accepted the idea that my
son may be dead, but his mother and I have to know for
sure."

"I can understand that, but what makes you think he
might be dead?" I asked.

"I know my son. We have always been close. He
would not simply disappear without a trace. That is not like
him."

"Are you sure?"

"Yes," he replied firmly.

* * * * * * *

Other titles by J.E. Terrall

Western Short Stories	Western Novels
The Old West	Conflict in Elkhorn Valley
The Frontier	Lazy A Ranch
Untamed Land	(A Modern Western)
Tales from the Territory	The Story of Joshua Higgins

Romance Novels	Mystery/Suspense/Thriller
Balboa Rendezvous	I Can See Clearly
Sing for Me	The Return Home
Return to Me	The Inheritance
Forever Yours	

Nick McCord Mysteries
Vol – 1 Murder at Gill's Point
Vol – 2 Death of a Flower
Vol – 3 A Dead Man's Treasure
Vol – 4 Blackjack, A Game to Die For
Vol – 5 Death on the Lakes
Vol – 6 Secrets Can Get You Killed

Peter Blackstone Mysteries	Frank Tidsdale Mysteries
Murder in the Foothills	Death by Design
Murder on the Crystal Blue	Death by Assassination
Murder of My Love	

SECRETS CAN GET YOU KILLED

A Nick McCord Mystery

Vol 6

by
J.E. Terrall

ISBN:978-0-9963951-4-4

This is a work of fiction. Names, characters, and incidents are either a product of the author's imagination or are used fictitiously, and any resemblance to actual persons, living or dead, is purely coincidental.

Printed in the United States of America
First Printing / 2013 – www.lulu.com
Second Printing / 2015 – www.createspace

Cover: Front and back covers done by author, J.E Terrall

Book Layout/
Formatting: J.E. Terrall
              Custer, South Dakota

SECRETS CAN GET YOU KILLED

To Stacy
Thank you for her encouragement and
support, and for being such a great neighbor

CHAPTER ONE

It was the kind of day that made you want to kick back, put your feet up, wrap you hands around a warm cup of coffee and relax. It had been raining all afternoon and showed no signs of letting up anytime soon. If it turned much colder, there was a good possibility of a few snowflakes; but it was unlikely that any of it would stick to the ground. The ground and pavement were still warm from several days of nice sunny, warm weather. According to the weatherman, it should warm up again.

Monica was busy in the kitchen fixing something for dinner. I had no idea what she was making; but if it was half as good as it smelled, it would be a very good meal. It crossed my mind that she could be very domestic if she wanted to be, and I liked it when she wanted to be.

As for me, I was in our home office looking out the window watching the rain slowly slide down the panes of glass in the window. I had just finished writing a letter to the President of Great Lakes Cruise Lines telling him what I expected the outcome of the trial of Andrew Thorndike would be, and where he was being held until his trial. I thanked them for the check covering our fees and expenses while working on a case for the cruise line. I also thanked him for the free passes for a cruise around the Great Lakes anytime we wanted to go.

The letter was ready to mail, but I was in no hurry to go out in the rain and cold to mail it. It could wait until the next time I had to go out. I was about to get up and go to the kitchen to see what smelled so good when the phone began to ring. It was the phone that we used for business. I reached over and picked up the receiver.

"McCord Detective Agency. How may I help you?"

"Is this Nick McCord?"

"Yes, it is."

"Mr. McCord, I would like to meet with you as soon as possible."

I had no idea who was on the other end of the line, but he sounded as if he expected me to drop whatever I was doing and bow to his order, which was not about to happen. However, he did catch me a little off guard. After a short pause, he continued.

"My son has been missing for five years, and no one seems to be able to find even the slightest trace of him."

"Before we get into that, I would like to know who you are, sir?" I asked interrupting him.

"Oh, I'm sorry. My name is Neil J. Cox."

"Well, Mr. Cox, finding people is the kind of work we do, but I must tell you that this kind of case often ends up unsolved. The older the case, the harder it is to solve. The longer a case goes unsolved, the more difficult it becomes to find clues that would help us find your son. Then there's the problem of finding witnesses that are reliable. That makes it almost impossible in older cases like what you are talking about. Five years is a long time in a missing person case."

"I understand that, but I'm willing to pay whatever it costs for you to find him, or at the very least, find out what happened to my son."

"Sir, it is often not a matter of money. Assuming that your son is alive; if he doesn't wish to be found, it becomes almost impossible to find him."

"Mr. McCord, I have already accepted the idea that my son may be dead, but his mother and I have to know for sure."

"I can understand that, but what makes you think he might be dead?" I asked.

"I know my son. We have always been close. He would not simply disappear without a trace. That is not like him."

"Are you sure?"

"Yes," he replied firmly.

"This case is pretty cold."

"I understand that, really I do. Would you at least meet with me so we can discuss it? I'll give you all the information I have from former investigators and from the police reports. I'm willing to pay you whatever your going rate is just for your time to discuss it and to have you look at the information I have, even if you decide not to go any further. I really need to have you look over what evidence I have before you make a decision. Would you please at least meet with me?" he begged.

I couldn't help but think that Mr. Cox needed to find someone who would take a real interest in looking for his son. It was a case that would probably turn out to be a deadend. It would not be easy, and more importantly, it might not give him the closure he was seeking no matter how much it would end up costing him. On the other hand, I had always liked a challenge, and this would certainly be a challenge.

"Before I agree to meet with you, I want to know how did you find me, Mr. Cox?"

"A friend of mine recommended you."

"What is your friend's name?"

I wasn't about to meet with him without something to convince me that he was worth my time and effort.

"Sam Bradford recommended you. You know him, I believe."

"Yes, I know him."

"He told me that you are a first rate investigator, and you wouldn't "skin me", as he so delicately put it."

I smiled at his comment. I remembered working with Sam awhile back at Knollwood's Resort and Casino in Ledyard, Connecticut. Sam was first rate in my book. There was no doubt that a quick call to him might be in order, if for no other reason than, to find out a little about Mr. Cox.

"I'll tell you what I'll do. I'll talk it over with my partner. If we decide that we are interested in learning more about your case, I'll call you back. I want to be right up front with you. If we decide to look into this for you, we make no guarantees that we will find your son. There will be no guarantees that we will even find out what happened to him. Is that understood?"

"Yes. Yes, it is. Thank you. Thank you very much," he replied with a sigh of relief I could hear over the phone.

"What is your son's full name?"

"William Jefferson Cox. He's named after his Great Grandfather," Mr. Cox said with a hint of pride in his voice.

"Don't get your hopes up too high, Mr. Cox," I warned him. "This case is pretty old. What is your phone number where we can reach you?"

He gave me his phone number. The area code was one of several in the New York City area. I would have to look it up to find out just what part of New York City.

"I'll get back to you later tonight," I assured him. "I expect you will be at this number?"

"Yes. I will be waiting for your call, and thank you."

I hung up just as Monica was coming into the office. She stopped at the door and leaned against the door frame. The look on her face told me that she wanted to know who had called.

"That was a call from a man who said his name was Cox, Neil J. Cox."

"Neil Cox of the Long Island, New York, Coxes?"

"Could be, why? He gave me a phone number that would be from the New York City area. Do you know who he is?" I asked.

"Yes, if he is the Neil Cox that I've heard of, he is a very rich man. He is also one of the most notable and respected dealers in rare antiques on the east coast. What did he want with us?"

"He wants us to try to find his son who has been missing for five years."

"Wow. What took him so long to get help finding his son?"

"From what he said, it sounded like he had help in the past, but with little or no results. I'm going to give Sam Bradford a call."

"Why call him?" Monica asked with a confused look on her face.

"The guy claims that Sam recommended us. Maybe I can find out a little about this guy. It would be nice to know if he is the same Neil Cox that you know."

"I don't really know Mr. Cox, but I know his reputation as a fair man, and a man that is widely known and respected in his field. Calling Sam sounds like a good idea. I'll leave you to make your call. Try not to take too long. Dinner is almost ready," she said, then left the office to return to the kitchen.

It took me a minute to find Sam's phone number at Knollwood's Resort and Casino. A quick glance at the clock on the wall told me it might be too late to get him at his office because of the time difference between the east coast and Wisconsin, but I decided to try anyway. The phone rang five times before it was answered.

"Knollwood's Security. How may I help you?" a woman's voice asked.

"This is Nick McCord. Does Sam happen to be in?"

"Yes, Mr. McCord. He's still here. I'll put you through to him."

"Thank you."

I didn't have to wait very long before Sam came on the line.

"Nick, how are you?"

"I'm fine. What about you?"

"I'm doing okay. And how is Monica?"

"She's fine, too."

"Well, I'm sure you didn't call for small talk. What's on our mind, Nick?"

"I was wondering if you know a Neil J. Cox?"

"I sure do. Did he call you?" Sam asked.

"As a matter of fact, he did. He called me about his missing son and said you suggested he call me to look into it for him."

"I did. William Cox is, or was Neil's son. About five years ago he went missing. Neil has hired all sorts of investigators and private eyes in an effort to find him. He has hounded the police for years to get them to keep looking into his missing son's case, but with little results," Sam explained.

"What made you recommend us? There has to be investigators in your area that could help him."

"Neil has tried about everyone he could to find his son. He was getting pretty desperate. He was here one afternoon visiting with me. I'm not really sure why he was here, but in the course of our conversation he told me about his frustration in trying to find his son. I suggested that if he was not satisfied with anyone here in the east, that he should contact you.

"Some of the investigators he has used in the past have done nothing but take his money and did little or nothing to earn it. I did a little checking into a few of the ones he had hired and found them to be not the most honest people in the business, you might say."

"What about Cooper?" I asked. "He seems to know his way around that part of the country, certainly a lot better than I do. Couldn't he help?"

"I called Cooper on Neil's behalf. When I explained the circumstances to Cooper, he agreed with me that I should have Neil contact you. Cooper said he was good at surveillance and that sort of thing, but missing persons was not his "forte", as he put it. He did say that if you took the case, he would be glad to help you in any way you believe he could."

"That was nice of him. Cooper's a good man. I haven't decided if we will take the case or not. These old cases are difficult and require a lot of time and effort. They can end up costing a lot of money and not produce any results."

"The one thing I do know is that Neil will pay you well for anything you can do for him. I told him that you were not cheap, so he expects to pay for your services. I also told him that you were good at what you do. If you couldn't find his son, it was very unlikely anyone else could."

"Thanks for the recommendation. Neil told me that he would pay me for my time just to discuss the case and to look over whatever information and evidence he has on it. It sounded like he might have a lot of information," I said.

"I'll tell you this much, Nick, if you look over the material he has from the previous investigators and the police, you'll take the case," Sam said.

"Why's that? Have you seen what he has on it?"

"I've seen some of it. Neil has not had very good results in the past. You will see that a number of what I think were good leads were never followed up by the investigators he had hired, or by the police. You may not ever find his son; but at least with someone like you on the case, he'll know that someone had made an honest effort."

"You wouldn't happen to be buttering me up so I'll take the case, would you?" I asked with a chuckle.

"No. Neil and I have been friends for a good many years. I guess I'm asking you to at least take a look at what he has as a favor to me. I would like to see someone who will take a real interest in finding his son and try to help him. William was his only son. In fact, he was his only child."

"I'll think about it," I assured him.

"That's all I'm asking you to do, and that's all he's asking you to do."

"I'll let you know what we decide. Right now, I have to have a talk with Monica."

"Good. Give her my best. If you get out this way, stop in and see me," Sam said.

"Will do," I said before I hung up.

I sat staring at the phone for a moment or two. This could prove to be one of the hardest cases I've ever worked on. I could see a lot of problems in finding William Cox. The major one being that the case was old. The longer it takes to resolve a case, the harder it is to find answers.

"Dinner's on," I heard Monica call from the kitchen.

I looked toward the door for a second or two before getting up and going to the kitchen. My mind was full of thoughts about what we could expect if we took on this case, but there was no way of knowing without finding out what Neil Cox had for evidence.

"What did you find out?" Monica asked as she set our dinner on the table.

"Nothing really, except that Sam would like us to talk to Cox, and look at the reports and evidence he has from the police and other investigators before we decide if we want to take it on."

"Why? What is Sam's interest in this?" she asked looking a little confused.

"Neil apparently has been a friend of his for sometime. Sam said that if we saw the evidence Cox had, we wouldn't be able to turn him down," I said as I sat down at the table.

"Maybe we should take a look at what he has and talk to him about it. It certainly couldn't hurt to have fresh eyes look at it," Monica said as she looked at me.

I looked at her while I took a minute to think about what she had said. I had to admit that deep down I was becoming more and more interested in the case based on what little I knew about it. Sam was not the kind of person who would lead me into something he didn't think was right. I couldn't help but think that it would be a challenge, and I have always liked a challenge.

"Okay," I said. "I'll call him back after dinner and make the arrangements to meet with him and look at what he has on the case."

Monica smiled at me, then we began to eat. The meal was as good as it smelled. We ate without talking very much. It seemed that we were both wondering what Mr. Cox could have that would make us want to work for him. When dinner was over, I started to help clear the table.

"I think you should call Mr. Cox," Monica said. "I'm sure he is chomping at the bit waiting to hear from us. I'll take care of the kitchen."

I kissed Monica on the cheek then went into the office and placed a call to Mr. Cox. The phone rang only once before it was picked up. He must have been sitting right next to it waiting for me to call him back.

"Hello?"

"Is this Mr. Neil Cox?"

"Yes, Mr. McCord."

"I want it understood that we make no promises, but my partner and I will take a look at the evidence and reports that you have. After that we will decide if we want to go any further."

"Oh, that's great."

I could hear the excitement as well as the relief in his voice. The last thing I wanted to do was to build his hopes up too high.

"Where would you like to meet?" I asked.

"I have a very large house here on Long Island. You can stay here while you look over what I have, if that's all right with you?"

"That would be fine."

"I will pick up all the costs for you to fly out here and for your return. I will provide you with whatever you need as well as pay your usual fees while you are here."

"That will be fine. There will be two of us."

"Of course. Sam said you have a female partner that you work with."

"Yes. She is not only my partner, she is my wife."

"Oh. Would you like me to arrange for your flight out here for the two of you?"

"That will not be necessary. We will make our own arrangements. I need you to understand that we will bill you for our expenses and fees for coming out to talk to you when we get there. Should we decide to take on the case, we will expect a retainer. We can explain all that when we get there, unless you would like that information now."

"That won't be necessary. I understand. If you let me know when you will be arriving, I'll have a car pick you up at the airport."

"If you don't mind, we would just as soon rent a car. We'll want to visit with some of the investigators and the police before we decide if we want go any further. We can do that on our way to your home."

"I understand. I'm sure your ability to move around as you deem necessary is important to you and the investigation. When might I expect you here at the house?"

"We should arrive in a couple of days. We will call you before we come out to your home."

"I will have everything ready for you. I look forward to meeting you in person, and thank you for taking the time to visit me and look at what I have regarding my son's disappearance."

"You're welcome," I said then hung up the phone.

Shortly after I hung up, Monica got on the phone and made arrangements for our flight to New York City. I got on the computer and began looking up everything that I could find on Neil J. Cox and his son, William J. Cox. It didn't take Monica long before she had a flight scheduled for us to leave just shortly after twelve the next day.

"We're all set. We will be flying first class and should arrive at Newark, New Jersey, just after five in the evening Newark time. I also lined up a car and a hotel room in Manhattan close to the Lincoln Center."

"Good. We can drive out to Long Island when we're ready."

"How are you doing?" she asked as she looked over my shoulder at the computer screen.

"I found some information on Neil Cox, but nothing on William, so far," I said.

I continued my search. It wasn't long before I ran onto an article that was from the New York Times dated about four months before William Cox disappeared. It was actually about Neil Cox and the fact that there had been a robbery at the Cox Estate. There had been a number of very old and expensive pieces of jewelry stolen from the estate. The article was just a little over five years old.

I continued the search for anything else that might be of interest. An article dated just two months after the robbery indicated that William had been arrested for drunk driving in Connecticut. He had apparently been returning from Ledyard, Connecticut, after a weekend at Knollwood's

Resort and Casino. That bit of information made it clear that Sam Bradford not only knew Neil Cox, but probably knew William as well.

Another article dated only a couple of days after William disappeared indicated that Neil had filed a missing person report on William. I wondered if there was any connection between the robbery and his disappearance, even though there was no apparent connection.

I was beginning to think that it might be a good idea if I had another talk with Sam. The question that passed through my mind was had Sam had any problems with William at Knollwood's? Based on what I had found out so far, there was a good chance that William might have had a gambling problem as well as a drinking problem, but neither had been confirmed. It would be something that I would have to look into.

I made a couple of notes of things I wanted to ask Sam about, then shut down the computer. I went into the bedroom where I found Monica busy gathering clothes and personal items to take with us.

"Did you find anything interesting?" she asked.

"Just that Cox apparently liked to gamble and drink."

"Which Cox?"

"William."

"Not a good combination," Monica said.

"No, it's not. They are two things that can get a person into a lot of trouble real fast."

"Do you think that might have something to do with his disappearance?"

"It might. But I'll save judgment on that until after I've seen what Neil has for evidence and what we find out about William from Sam and the police."

"Sounds like a good idea," Monica said.

I got our suitcases and began putting everything into them. There was no sense packing a gun since I wouldn't be able to get it on board the plane. Besides, I doubted that I would need a gun.

As soon as we were packed, I set the suitcases aside. I took a shower then crawled into bed while I waited for Monica to join me. When she returned to the bedroom, I was lying on my back with my hands behind my head staring up at the ceiling.

"What are you thinking about?" Monica asked.

"I was thinking about us."

"What about us?" she asked as she crawled under the covers and curled up beside me.

"I was thinking about the last time we were on the east coast. Things got a little tense at times."

"You're not thinking about leaving me behind, are you?"

"No. I wouldn't do that to you. We're partners. Besides, we are just going to take a look and see if we want to pursue this case."

"I think you already know that we are," she said with a grin.

"I think you're right. Now, what was that about getting some sleep?"

She smiled and rolled up against me. I tucked her close to me. We did a little necking and petting before we curled up against each other and went to sleep.

CHAPTER TWO

I found myself wide awake well before the alarm was due to wake us. My mind was filled with thoughts of William Cox. I didn't have much information on him, but I got the impression he might have gotten into some kind of trouble that was way over his head. I knew that he apparently liked to drink and gamble. Not a good thing. It might take a bit of investigating to find out how deep William was into both, and to whom he might owe money.

Monica was lying beside me and still sleeping. I started to mentally go over in my mind who I wanted to visit with before we went out to Long Island to talk to Mr. Cox, and begin to review what evidence he had gathered over the years.

I needed to know what went on in William's life for, say, the six months to a year prior to his disappearance. That time could provide a good deal of information on what he was into that either made him want to disappear or caused his disappearance. It could also help me get a little insight into William's character and what made him tick before I talked to his father.

A background check on William was also something we should look into. His past could prove not only interesting, but might give us an idea of what he was doing before he dropped out of sight.

"You ready to get up?" Monica asked, interrupting my thoughts.

"Sure. I've got an idea on how to get a background check on William."

"How?" she asked as she got out of bed.

"I'll give Sergeant Wallace a call and ask him to run a background check on William. He can get information from other police agencies around the country that might not be so easy for me to get."

"Good idea. Why don't you do that while I fix breakfast?"

"Okay."

After getting dressed, I went into our home office and placed a call to the Milwaukee Police Department. The phone was answered almost immediately.

"Milwaukee Police Department, Fifth Precinct, how may I help you?"

"You can help me a lot, Frank."

"Nick? That you?"

"Sure is."

"It's been a while since I've heard from you. How are things going?"

"Pretty good. How are things going with you?"

"Good. Say, did you ever marry that sexy blond you were so hung up on?" Frank asked with a chuckle.

"I sure did."

"Good for you. What can I do for you?"

"I was wondering if you could do a background check on a William Jefferson Cox? He has been missing for about five years. He's from Long Island, New York. He's the son of Neil J. Cox. He may have been arrested by the Connecticut police for drunk driving, so they may have something on him. That's about all I have at the moment."

"I'll send out an inquiry to New York and the surrounding states and see what I can get for you. Where do you want me to send what I get?"

"I'll be in New York by tonight, but I don't know how long we'll be there. How about if I give you a call in a couple of days and tell you where to send it?"

"Sure, that'll work. If you're going to be in New York, why not have the New York police get the background check for you?"

"I don't know anyone there, and I don't know how cooperative they will be with an out-of-state PI."

"I see your point. Tell you what, when you get there you might look up a sergeant by the name of Marcus Longmont. He works out of one of the Manhattan precincts. He's an old friend of mine; and if I recall, he attended one of your classes on preserving evidence. He may feel that he already knows you. He works out of the Twelfth Precinct. I'll give him a heads up. In the meantime, I'll do what I can."

"Thanks. By the way, how's the wife?" I asked.

"Still nagging me to retire. I think she's winning," Frank said with a chuckle. "I'm planning to hang up the badge the first of the year."

"Good for you. You've put in enough time. Let me know when you have your retirement party, Monica and I would like to come."

"I'd like that. I'll let you know. Say "Hi" to Monica for me."

"Will do."

"Give our best to Jane," I said.

"I'll do that. Take care out there. It's a hard world."

"We will. Talk to you later," I said then hung up.

As I sat there looking at the phone and thinking, the smell of breakfast drifted into the office. I got up and walked out to the kitchen to find Monica dishing up a ham and cheese omelet. She looked up and smiled.

"Did you get hold of Sergeant Wallace?"

"Yes. He gave me the name of a friend of his in New York City who could prove to be helpful. He's a cop there."

"That could be helpful. Sit down. Breakfast is ready."

"By the way, Frank plans to hang it up the first of the year, and he said to say "Hi"."

"It's about time for him to retire. I know Jane will be glad he's out of there," Monica said.

We sat down and ate our breakfast, and cleaned up the kitchen together. Once that was done, we finished packing what we planned to take to New York and loaded it in my car. We drove to the Milwaukee airport and left my car there.

* * * *

The flight to Newark, New Jersey airport was uneventful. We arrived a few minutes early and went right to the car rental area after getting our luggage. It was only a matter of minutes and we were on our way. We left New Jersey by way of the Holland Tunnel which took us directly into Manhattan. Not being all that familiar with Manhattan, it took us a little while to find our hotel.

We checked in after parking our car in the underground garage. It was a very nice hotel with all the conveniences anyone could ask for. The bellhop escorted us to our room and carried in our luggage.

"Say, could you tell me where the Twelfth Precinct of the New York Police Department is located?"

The bellhop looked at me as if I was crazy, but smiled and told me how to get there from the hotel. It turned out that it was not very far. He also suggested that I might want to walk or take a cab as it was difficult to find a place to park a car in the city.

I thanked him for the information then gave him a tip. He thanked me then left our room.

"What are you thinking? Are you planning on going there now?"

"It's too late to go tonight. We can go first thing in the morning and see if we can find Frank's friend. Right now, I would like to go to the restaurant and get some dinner. We can start looking into things tomorrow."

"I like that idea," Monica said.

We spent the next half hour or so to freshen up. We were ready to leave our hotel room when the phone rang. As I walked across the room to answer the phone, I wondered who could be calling us. I hadn't told anyone where we would be staying.

"Hello."

"Is this Nick McCord?"

"Yes, it is."

"I'm Sergeant Longmont, Sergeant Marcus Longmont. A mutual friend of ours said you would be coming to New York and would be interested in talking to me."

"That is correct. We would like to get together and visit with you about William Cox, if you don't mind?"

"Are you busy now? We could meet tonight if it would be convenient?"

"We were just about to leave to get something to eat."

"Good. There's a little restaurant two blocks south of the front entrance to your hotel. They have great steaks there. What do you say we meet there in about fifteen minutes?"

"Sounds good. We'll see you there. How will I know you?"

"I'll know you," he said.

"Okay."

As the phone went dead, I looked over at Monica. The look on her face told me that she was wondering what was going on.

"That was Sergeant Marcus Longmont."

"The policeman we were going to contact?"

"Yes."

"How did he know where to find us?"

"I'm not sure, but you can ask him. Frank probably told him we were coming to New York, and he called around to the hotels to find out where we were going to be staying. We are having dinner with him very shortly. You ready to go?"

"Sure."

We left the hotel and started walking down the street toward the restaurant Longmont had told us about. I could tell by the look on Monica's face that she was concerned about something.

"What's on your mind, honey?"

"It seems a little strange to me that a police officer would call us and want to meet us at a restaurant. Why wouldn't he want to meet with us at the police station or even in our hotel room?"

"I don't know, but maybe he just wants to welcome us to New York. After all, he is a friend of Frank Wallace who is a friend of ours."

"I suppose you're right. Maybe I'm just a bit suspicious."

"That's not all bad. I have a few doubts about what we are getting into here, too. It certainly doesn't hurt to be a bit suspicious. It tends to make us a little more careful."

It was about the time Longmont had suggested that we arrive at the restaurant. We turned and went inside. It was only a minute or so before we were seated in a booth. We were immediately served a glass of water and given a menu. We told the waiter that we were waiting for someone and would wait until he arrived to order.

I looked around the restaurant. It was a nice clean place. It had the look of a late nineteenth century restaurant. There was a lot of dark woodwork, fancy old styled lights, and lots of mirrors. The walls had a good number of nineteenth century paintings, and red and gold flocked wallpaper.

We took a few minutes to look the menu over. It seemed a little pricey, but if the food was good, it would be worth it. Thinking back to my days on the force, this didn't strike me as the type of place that a cop would frequent.

"Nick."

I looked up at Monica. She was looking toward the front door. I turned my head and looked toward the door. There was a tall black man standing just inside the door. He was looking around the restaurant as if looking for someone. When his eyes met mine, he smiled and started across the room toward us.

"Don't get up," he said as he walked up to the booth. "I'm Sergeant Longmont."

"I'm Nick McCord," I said as I motioned for him to sit across from us. "And this is my wife, Monica."

"Nice to meet you both."

"I take it Frank called you and told you we might be looking you up while we are here."

"That's right. He said that you were looking into the - - - -" he said, but stopped when the waiter showed up.

We ordered dinner then waited for the waiter to leave.

"As I was saying, Frank said that you were looking into the William Cox case. You realize that case is still open?"

"We didn't, but we are aware that it has not been resolved."

"It is still open, but it is not being actively investigated at the moment by the department. All the leads we have had dried up or have gone cold."

"Mr. Cox, Neil, seems to think he has some evidence that was not followed up on by either the police or by the private investigators he hired. You've obviously looked over the evidence. Do you agree with him?"

"No, at least as far as the evidence we have is concerned. I'm not sure what evidence some of Mr. Cox's last investigators may have found. Private investigators don't often share with us. Since we were not able to find his son, he has not been in touch with us for the past couple of years. I guess you would say that he more or less gave up on us. He didn't seem to believe we were giving him our undivided attention."

"I understand," I said, then waited when I saw our waiter coming toward us.

I sat back while the waiter put our salads down in front of us. I noticed that Longmont watched the waiter very closely. It seemed he watched him with more interest than I would have expected. I got the feeling that he might know the waiter and didn't trust him. Either that or he didn't want him to hear what we were talking about.

"Most people don't realize that they are not the only case a police department has to work on, or at least they feel their case is not getting the attention it should. In most departments, when a case goes on as long as this one has, they tend to pull back a little to work on more current cases that have some hot leads that need to be followed up quickly."

"That's right, but we have given this as much attention as personnel will allow. Every lead we had we followed up, but nothing came of any of them," Sergeant Longmont said.

"What can you tell me about William Cox?" I asked.

"I can tell you he has been arrested several times for driving under the influence, and he crashed his car twice while drunk."

"Over how long a period of time?"

Longmont again waited until the waiter had served our dinners before he continued.

"Over a period of about five or six months. Maybe a little longer."

"That seems like a pretty short time. Was there anything before that?"

"No. Not a thing. Before that his record was clean," Sergeant Longmont said.

"How long before his disappearance was that?"

"That was in the five months or so before he disappeared. Now that was just here in New York. He was also arrested for driving under the influence in Connecticut. He apparently was heading back to Long Island after what would be considered an unsuccessful trip to one of the large casinos up there," Sergeant Longmont explained.

"Would that be Knollwood's by any chance?" I asked.

"It could be, but it could have been any of the other large casinos. We don't know which casinos he liked to visit, or if he visited several."

"Did you follow up to see where he had been?"

"Not on his problems in Connecticut. All we have on those is what was in the reports we requested from the Connecticut police. All they said was that he had been gambling and drinking, and he had lost a good deal of money while he was in Connecticut. They didn't say where he had been gambling."

"I take it that was about the same time as his problems here in New York?"

"Yes."

"What about here in New York? Did he gamble here as well?" I asked.

"Yes," Sergeant Longmont replied. "It seems he liked racing, both dog and horse racing. He lost a good sum of money on the ponies over the five or six months before he disappeared."

"Any other gambling that you know about?" I asked.

"No, but that doesn't mean he didn't gamble illegally. My guess was that he had a serious gambling problem. We looked at his disappearance as maybe having something to do with his gambling, but we couldn't find any connection that we could prove. In fact, we came up empty on that theory."

"By looking into it, you tried to find out if he had been gambling illegally?"

"Yeah. Like I said, we came up empty. But that doesn't mean he wasn't gambling. It only means we didn't find any evidence that he was gambling illegally."

I looked over at Monica. She had been eating, but I was sure she hadn't missed a word that was said.

We finished our meal with a little small talk that was unimportant to our case. Sergeant Longmont left after telling us to call him if we had anything new that he could use. We agreed to contact him if we found anything.

After he left, we sat there and thought about what he had said. Everything he said made perfect sense. Yet, it still made me wonder how much effort they had given to finding William.

"What's our next move?" Monica asked interrupting my thoughts.

"A good night's sleep. Tomorrow, I think it would be a good idea if we drove up to Knollwood's and had a talk with Sam Bradford."

"Sounds good to me," Monica said with a smile.

We took our time walking back to the hotel. It wasn't long before we climbed into bed. It had been a very long day with the flight, and we were both tired. Sleep came quickly.

CHAPTER THREE

We woke the next morning fairly early. It was going to take a long time to get from New York City to Ledyard, Connecticut. There was little doubt in my mind that traffic in the Big Apple would be heavy. We checked out of the hotel and headed for the interstate that would take us to Connecticut.

"I got the impression from Detective Longmont that William's disappearance might have something to do with his gambling," Monica said. "Do you think that is the case?"

"I don't know, but it's beginning to look like it might be. I'm hoping that Sam will be able to shed some light on it."

Monica sat looking out the window of the car as I drove. I had no idea what she was thinking about, but it probably had to do with William Cox.

"How long do you think we will be at Knollwood's?"

"I don't know, but I wouldn't think it will be very long. Probably just overnight. Why?"

"I was thinking that it might be a good idea if we got a look at what Mr. Cox has for evidence before we go much further. He may have some evidence that will give us a clue why William Cox disappeared. Who knows who we might end up dealing with," Monica said as she turned her head and looked at me.

"You have a very good point, but what I'm looking for now is a little background on William before we start looking into his disappearance. I want to know as much as possible about William and his activities in the five to six months before he disappeared. There might be things that his father doesn't know about or isn't telling us about.

"There may be things he did that would help us understand the evidence Mr. Cox has a little better. It may also help us decide what evidence Mr. Cox has that is of value and what is useless information," I explained.

"In other words, evidence doesn't mean anything if we don't know how it fits into the bigger picture."

"I wouldn't say it doesn't mean anything, but its value to pointing us in the right direction and the final outcome of the investigation may not be much. There's a better than average chance that Mr. Cox will have, shall we say, a slanted view of his son and his activities. He may not have told us things we need to know, either on purpose or by accident."

"I see. You are good at what you do," she said with a smile.

"Well, thank you," I replied. "You are good at what you do, too."

It was almost noon when we arrived at Knollwood's Resort and Casino. We parked our rented car in the parking lot and walked into the Casino. Nothing had changed much. People were dropping money in those noisy machines almost as fast as they could. There were bells and whistles going off as we walked toward the tower where the hotel was located. Arriving at the hotel desk, we were greeted by a well dressed man in his mid-to-late fifties.

"May I help you, sir?" he asked.

"Yes. Do you have a room available for just tonight?"

"Do you have reservations, sir?"

"No, I'm afraid not."

"I have a small suite available if that would be all right?"

"That would be fine."

The man put a card on the counter then said, "Would you fill this out, please."

I filled out the card and slid it back across the counter to him. He looked at it then smiled.

"It is good to have you visit us again, Mr. McCord. Would you like me to contact Mr. Bradford for you, or would you rather go to your room first?"

"You may call him and let him know we are here. By the way, how did you know we were here to see him?"

"Mr. Bradford said that you might be coming by."

"Oh."

The man smiled, then turned and picked up the phone and placed a call. He spoke for just a minute or so then hung up.

"Mr. Bradford said that he will meet you in the Veranda Café in about ten minutes."

"Thank you."

"If you leave your luggage here, I will see that it is taken to your room for you," he said as he handed me the key card to our room.

"Thank you," I said then turned to Monica.

I took Monica by the arm and led her away from the desk. We walked over to the elevators.

I pressed the button, then stepped back to wait. Several people moved up close to the elevator to wait. When the elevator arrived we stepped inside then waited for the others to get in the elevator. When all were in, I pressed the button for the Mezzanine Level where the Veranda Café was located and pressed the buttons to other floors as the other passengers called out the floor number they wanted.

When we arrived at the floor we wanted, the elevator stopped and we stepped off. We walked down the hall toward the café. Just as we were about to enter the café, we saw Sam coming toward us.

"It's good to see the two of you again," Sam said as he stuck out his hand.

"It's good to see you, too," I said as I shook his hand.

"Come in," he said as he pointed toward the café.

We entered the café and were immediately led to a booth in a corner. After sitting down, a waitress came over to get our order. Sam told the waitress that he was to get the bill, then we ordered.

"Well, what can I do to help you? I assume that you are here to find out as much about William Cox as you can."

"That's right."

"I can tell you that he was not a gambler," Sam said with a slight chuckle.

"What do you mean by that?"

"William used to come here – oh – about every two or three months to do a little recreational gambling," Sam began. "He would gamble at Blackjack and play a little on the slot machines. He would lose a couple of hundred dollars and then go home. He never caused any trouble. He was what we call a casual gambler. For him to lose a few hundred dollars a visit was not a big deal.

"But in the last five or six months before he disappeared, he would come much more often, maybe three or four times a month. He would often stay several nights during which time he would lose several thousand dollars. I can tell you that got the attention of some of my people. They reported it to me because they knew that I knew his father personally."

"What do you see as the reason for the change?" I asked.

"I don't know. I had to call Neil Cox, his father, a couple of times to come and get him. I even went so far as to suggest that William take his business elsewhere. I didn't want his gambling to ruin my friendship with Neil."

"Did he do that?"

"Did he gamble someplace else? I would have to say, yes. However, very shortly after I told him not to come back, he was reported missing," Sam said.

"How long was it between the time you told him not to come anymore and when he disappeared?"

"Not very long, maybe a week at the most. Maybe only a few days. I don't know for sure," Sam said.

"Have you looked at the videos of him gambling to see if there was anyone that might have been around him while he gambled?" I asked.

"You mean anyone that I thought might be watching him a little too closely?"

"Yeah, or someone who would walk by him several times in, say, thirty minutes."

"I looked, but didn't notice anyone."

"I take it you watched him fairly closely?"

"I didn't at first, but I did after he started losing large amounts of money."

"Did you ever have any trouble with him while he was here?"

"Only the last time he was here did I have any serious trouble with him. Before that, he would leave if asked to do so."

"What happened that last time?"

"He got into it with one of my security people."

"How so?"

"I told one of my security people to quietly take him away from the Blackjack table and escort him to his room. The three or four other times I had him removed from the tables he went quietly and didn't give my security people any trouble, but not the last time. He punched the security guard in the mouth and was immediately cuffed and brought to my office," Sam explained.

"What did you do then?"

"I should have arrested him for drunk and disorderly, and for assaulting one of my security guards, but I didn't. The guard was not hurt very bad, plus being a friend of his father's, I didn't want to cause him to have a record. I called Neil and told him to come and get him. I also told him that he wasn't welcome here any more; and if he came back, he would be arrested on the spot."

"What did Neil have to say about that?"

"I think he was embarrassed by it all."

"Did his father come and get him?"

"Neil came to get him, but when he got here William was gone. We had escorted him to his room and posted a guard at the door just as we had done before. I guess my people were a little lax because we hadn't had any problem with him cooperating before. This time he overpowered the guard and took off in his car. I found out the next day from Neil that he had been picked up by the Connecticut State Police and was arrested for drunk driving. As far as I know, Neil went and bailed him out the morning after he was arrested," Sam explained.

"Was that when he disappeared?"

"No. He disappeared a couple of days after that."

"Did William say anything that was strange or out of the ordinary for him when you detained him?"

"He was pretty drunk when we removed him from the Blackjack table the last time. His words were slurred. He was hard to understand."

"Didn't any of your dealers realize he was drunk," I asked, a little surprised that they would let him gamble if he was drunk.

"I questioned them about it, then looked at the tapes from the table where he played. You have to remember that in Blackjack you don't have to say anything to play. You can tell the dealer what you want with hand movements. He didn't say a word and he sat up straight. On the tapes he looked as sober as you or me. He didn't do anything to make the dealer think that he might have had too much to drink. I'm sure that if he spoke, the dealer would have known immediately he was drunk."

"I guess that doesn't help me much."

"I'm sorry, Nick. If you would like, I can get you the tapes of the last three times he was here. Maybe you will see something I missed."

I looked at Monica. She nodded that it might be a good idea if we looked at them since we were already there.

"Okay. I don't know what help they will be, but it certainly can't hurt."

"Meet me in my office in about twenty minutes. I'll have them set up a TV so you can review them. I'll have some coffee brought in."

"Thanks," I said as I watched him stand up.

Sam left the café while Monica and I finished our coffee. I don't know what was going on in Monica's head, but I was wondering why the sudden change in William's gambling habits. Was it just a case of him becoming more addicted to gambling and needed to satisfy his addiction, or was there something else behind it?

"What are you thinking?" Monica asked.

"I'm not sure."

"I can understand that. What made him change so quickly? People don't normally go from a casual gambler to a fanatical gambler so quickly. It's usually a gradual increase in gambling to the point where it finally consumes them."

"I agree, but something had to make him change so quickly. I want to know what it was," I said as I looked at her.

"I had a thought. Maybe he didn't change all that quickly. Maybe he had been doing a lot of gambling in other places. Think about it. If he had been cut off from the other places he liked to gamble, it might have forced him to do more gambling here. Wouldn't that explain the sudden change?" Monica asked as she looked to me for answers.

There was no doubt that she had a valid point. It was a possibility, but there was something else that made me think that was not the case. Everything we had found out so far seemed to point to the change in him had occurred over just the five months or so before he disappeared.

"What about the fact that his actions seemed to have changed in only the five months before he disappeared? Wouldn't that indicate the sudden change in his life was caused by something other than his gambling? Maybe some outside pressure, or something that he had a problem dealing with," I said.

"Any ideas as to what it might have been?"

"I hate to think it, but it could have been drugs."

"You might be right," Monica said after a moment of thought. "Maybe we should go take a look at the tapes."

"Okay," I said as I got up from the table.

I pulled Monica's chair back as she stood up, then took her hand. We left the café and headed for Sam's Office.

* * * *

When we arrived, Sam had a pot of coffee and a couple of cups on the table. There was also a fairly large TV with a VCR set up in the corner.

"It's ready," Sam said.

"Switch it on," I said as I sat down next to Monica.

"Each tape is about two hours long."

"How many are there?"

"Five. Two of them show him playing the slots. The rest are of him playing Blackjack. I'll play the three for the Blackjack tables. The first one is from the next to the last time he was here. That would have been about a week before he disappeared. The second is from the day before I asked him not to come back. And the third one is when I had him removed from the Blackjack table. So here goes."

Monica and I watched the first tape. It started out showing William coming to the Blackjack table and sitting down. He seemed to be in complete control of what he was doing. I did notice that he had several drinks in the two hours of tape, but he didn't seem to be effected by it. I took notice of the young woman who served him as well as anyone in the background that I could see. I saw nothing that would cause me to get suspicious.

The second tape was taken at the same Blackjack table. Again, it seemed that he was in complete control of every move he made. I did notice that he never said a word. He was served drinks by the same woman who had served him in the first tape. Otherwise, nothing seemed to be out of the ordinary.

"Stop the tape," Monica blurted out.

"Did you see something?" I asked as Sam stopped the tape.

"I think so. Look at the upper right hand corner of the screen. You can't see the guys face, but the jacket is the same as the one in the previous tape. If you look closely, the fancy belt buckle is the same, too. It could be someone who was watching him."

I looked at the screen. Sure enough, there was someone standing behind William. He was far enough back that his face was not visible.

"Let's see if he turns up in the last tape." I suggested.

"We will be leaving in the morning. I would like you to take a look at all the tapes you can find on William. I want to know when he started playing at that particular table, and how often the same man was standing behind him. I also want to know if the same woman served him drinks and the same woman dealt the cards," I said to Sam.

"You think there was something going on?" Sam asked.

"I don't know, but it would be nice to find out."

"I'll take care of it."

"Is it normal for the same dealer to be at the same table all the time?" I asked.

"No. The pit boss usually has a rotating schedule for the dealers so they don't work at the same table or deal the same game all the time. They don't like the dealers to get too familiar with the customers," Sam explained.

"What about the cocktail waitresses?"

"They might work the same area. You still want to see the last tape?"

"Yes," I replied.

As the video came on the screen, I immediately saw the man with the same jacket and belt buckle standing behind William. Just as the young woman brought William a drink, I could see the green jacketed security guards come into view. I watched them as they approached William.

Since there was no audio, I couldn't hear what they were saying; but it was clear that they were asking William to leave the table and go with them. As William go off the chair, he took a swing and hit one of Sam's security guards. He was immediately wrestled to the floor, cuffed and taken away.

"I would like to see that over again. I watched what happened to William, now I would like to see what happened in the background," I said.

Sam ran the tape back, then restarted just a second or two before the security guards came into camera range. Watching the background, I noticed that the man in the jacket wearing the fancy belt buckle quickly backed away. I lost sight of him just as he turned around. I also noticed the young woman who had waited on William had suddenly disappeared as well.

"Sam, does that woman who served William drinks still work here?"

"I don't know, but I'll sure find out."

"When you do, you might want to question her about this incident. You might want to talk to the dealer as well."

"You got it. I'll let you know what I find out."

"Thanks. Any idea who the guy with the fancy belt buckle might be?"

"None, but I'll ask around," Sam assured me. "Maybe one of my people knows him or would be able to identify him for us."

"Good idea. I think Monica and I have had it for today. I think we'll go get something for dinner then return to our room. We have plenty to think about."

"Okay. What are you going to do tomorrow?" Sam asked.

"I think we will go see our client."

"Will you be staying at his place?"

"I would think so. He indicated that he has a lot of evidence. It will probably take us some time to go through all of it. We'll have to weed out what is useless and figure out what is useful."

"I'm sure it will. I'll call you there if I come up with anything."

"Thanks."

"Have a good night," Sam said as we left his office.

We returned to our suite. On the table was a large bowl of fresh fruits and a note welcoming us to Knollwood's Resort and Casino. We found our luggage had been neatly placed on the luggage rack in the bedroom.

"It was nice of them to leave us a bowl of fruit," Monica said.

"Yes, it was."

"Are you ready to go to bed?" she asked.

"I think so. We've had a long day and I suspect it will be another long day tomorrow."

"I would like a shower. How about you?" Monica asked.

"I would like that," I said with a grin.

We went into the large bathroom, undressed and got into the very large and very nice shower. We spent a lot of time necking and touching each other. We spent more time holding each other in the shower than we did washing. Her body felt so good up against me. I couldn't help but think that I was the luckiest man in world to be loved by such a beautiful and intelligent woman.

After a while, a long while, we got out of the shower and dried off. I was feeling very romantic. So I picked Monica up and carried her to the large bed. We spent the next hour or so making love to each other, then fell asleep in each other's arms.

CHAPTER FOUR

The alarm clock went off right on time, darn it. I wasn't really ready to get up, but we had another long day ahead of us. I turned my head and looked at Monica. She looked like she was wide awake. I have never seen a woman look so sexy this early in the morning.

"You ready to get up?" she asked.

"No, but I suppose we should. We have a lot to do."

Just then the phone began to ring. I looked at Monica, then reached over and picked up the receiver from the phone on the bedside table.

"Hello."

"Nick, this is Sam. I found out about the waitress. She only worked for us for about five months. She quit without notice the same night that William was taken away from the Blackjack table by security."

"Interesting."

"Yes, it is."

"What was her name?"

"Susan Small."

"Did she give a reason for quitting?" I asked.

"No. She just said she couldn't work here any longer. When asked for details, she refused to give a reason."

"Was she paid for her time when she quit?"

"We mailed her last check to her, but the post office returned it. We still have it."

"Where did she live?" I asked.

"The address she gave us was in Avery Hill, Connecticut."

Sam gave me the woman's name and address, and I wrote them down on a pad next to the phone.

"What about the dealer?"

She's still with us," Sam said. "She's been a dealer for over six years. We've never had any trouble with her. She has been an excellent employee and is up for a promotion."

"What does she have to say about working the same table so often?"

"She was working as a fill-in for a two month period back then, and simply drew that table. What she said was confirmed by the man who had been her pit boss at the time. Do you think she had something to do with it?" Sam asked.

"I don't know, but it's possible. How well do you trust her pit boss?"

"I trust him. He's been with us for a good many years."

"Then it's probably on the up and up. I will leave it at that unless something comes up to indicate otherwise."

"You will let me know if something comes up?" Sam asked.

"Sure thing."

"Okay. Will I see you later?"

"I'm not sure, but I will let you know what we decide on the Cox case."

"Good. I'll be here if you need me for anything. Have a safe trip."

"We will," I said then hung up.

"I take it that was Sam," Monica said as she came out of the bathroom. "Did he have anything to say about the waitress and the dealer?"

"It looks like the dealer's clean, but the waitress quit the same night Sam had William removed from the Blackjack table."

"That's interesting. What do you think it means?"

"I have no idea," I said thoughtfully. "It may mean nothing at all, or it may mean something. I did get an address for the waitress. We can check it out later if we decide it's important in finding William."

"What do we do now?"

"I think our next stop is Long Island, the Cox Estate."

Monica simply nodded that she agreed with me. I spent the next half hour getting ready to go get some breakfast before leaving Knollwood's.

We had a quiet breakfast in one of the cafés before we checked out. After tossing our luggage in the trunk of the rented car, we headed for Long Island.

* * * *

We arrived at the Cox Estate on Long Island shortly before noon. The large four story brick house sat way back from the road. It could only be described as a late nineteenth century mansion, typical of wealthy people like the Carnegies, Rockefellers and Vanderbilts. There was a brick wall across the front of the property along the road. It had a large iron gate with security cameras on either side. One was pointed where the driver of a car would be if he was at the intercom while the other was directed at the driveway area in front of the gate. I pulled up to the intercom and was about to press the button when a security guard came out of the guard building.

"How may I help you?" the guard asked.

"I'm Nick McCord and this is my wife Monica McCord. We are here to see Mr. Neil Cox."

"Thank you, Mr. McCord. Mr. Cox is expecting you. Please drive up the drive to the front of the house. You will be met there. Thank you."

"Thank you." I replied.

When the guard stepped back into the guardhouse, I turned and watched as the gate slowly opened. When it was opened enough to drive through, I drove up the long drive to the house. Just as I turned in front of the house, I saw a tall man who looked to be in his late fifties to early sixties. He was dressed in dark slacks and a white dress shirt with his collar open.

There was also a big man wearing a dark suit with the jacket open. He stood next to the older gentleman and never took his eyes off us. There was no doubt in my mind that he was a bodyguard.

I pulled to a stop, got out and walked around to the other side of the car. I opened the door and helped Monica out of the car.

"The guy in the white shirt is Cox," she whispered.

"Yeah. I figured that since the guy in the suit is carrying a gun under his left arm."

Monica looked at me for a second, then smiled. I took her hand and led her up the steps to the porch.

"Mr. McCord, it is nice to finally meet you in person."

"Nice to finally meet you, Mr. Cox," I said as I shook his hand.

"And you must be Monica. Sam said you were a beautiful young woman."

"Thank you, Mr. Cox," Monica said with a smile.

"Please come in."

He didn't wait for us to say anything. He simply turned around and went back inside the house. Once inside, he spoke to a fairly short, nice looking man with dark almost black eyes. He had a pleasant looking face. He was wearing a white jacket and stood next to the door.

"Would you please get Mr. and Mrs. McCord's luggage from their car and take it to the guestroom."

"Yes, sir," he said.

I handed the man the keys to the car, then followed Mr. Cox into the study. He motioned for us to have a seat, then sat down across the coffee table from us.

"I hope your trip was a pleasant one."

"Yes, it was," Monica replied.

"Good. I have set up the room next to this one for you to work out of. It has a phone for your use. I have also gathered all the papers and evidence that I have. I put it on the large table. I hope it will be adequate for you."

"I'm sure it will be fine," I said.

"Since I didn't know when you would be arriving, I didn't bother to reschedule a business meeting I have in New York City tomorrow. I will be gone most of the day."

"That shouldn't be any problem," I said. "From what you have told us, there will be plenty to keep us busy sorting through the reports and evidence you already have."

"Good. I'm sure you would like to freshen up before you start looking into my son's disappearance."

"To be honest with you, we have already started looking into it," I said.

"I was sure you had," he said with a smile. "Except for tomorrow, I should be available most of the week to answer any questions you might have. I have instructed my staff to be available at anytime to answer any questions you might have of them."

"Thank you," I said. "Your cooperation and the cooperation of your staff will be very helpful. I'm sure that you are well aware that honesty in answering our questions will be a big help in finding the truth and, hopefully, in finding your son."

"I understand. Will you be here for dinner?"

I looked at Monica before I answered.

"Yes. I doubt that we will have any questions until we have had a chance to look at some of the evidence you have. I was thinking we would like to freshen up, as you said, then we would like to get started."

"Tonight?"

"I'd like to start this afternoon, if you don't mind," I said.

"Not at all. Have you had lunch?"

"Not yet. We thought we would check in with you to let you know we were here, then go get something to eat before we start."

"That will not be necessary. I'll have some sandwiches made that we can eat while we discuss your fee and what you will need for a retainer."

"That would be very nice," Monica said.

"After lunch we would like to get started by going over what you have in the way of evidence and the reports from the investigators and police," I added.

"I guess I thought you would relax tonight and start in the morning."

"As I said before, we have already started, Mr. Cox. We've already talked to a couple of people."

"Ah – yes. You did tell me that. I see you waste no time."

I didn't reply to his comment, I simply smiled.

"I'll have Koato show you to your room. I'll meet you in this room in, say about, thirty minutes?"

"That would be fine," Monica said.

Neil got up and left the room. He had no more than disappeared when the man in the white coat who had been at the front door came into the study.

"Would you follow me, please," he said, then turned and left the room.

Monica and I followed him to a long spiral staircase. We walked up to the second floor and down a long hall where he stopped and opened a door.

"This will be your room while you are with us," Koato said. "If you should need anything, there is a white button on the table beside the bed. Simply press it and I will come to see what it is you need."

"Thank you. By the way, are you Koato?"

"Yes, sir."

"Would you mind answering a question for me?"

"Not at all. I have been instructed to be at your service while you are here."

"Were you working here when William lived here?"

"Yes, sir. I have been with the Cox family a little over thirty years."

"Thank you, Koato."

"Is there anything else?"

"Not at the moment. Thank you."

I watched as Koato nodded his head slightly, then turned and walked down the hall toward the stairs. As soon as he was gone, we went into the room. It was a magnificent room. It had ten foot high ceilings with walnut cross beams. The walls were paneled with walnut that had been polished to a glossy finish. The windows were tall and narrow with heavy drapes. There were several paintings on the walls and a couple of full length mirrors. The furniture in the room looked very old and beautiful. There was a four poster bed, a very large chest of drawers, and a dressing table, all in matching style and wood. The room was very impressive and tended to take one back in history to the early nineteenth or late eighteenth century. But Monica would know more about that than I.

"This is really something," I said as I looked around the room.

"It sure is. It is more like what you would find in a museum. This is some very expensive antique furniture. Most of what is in this room dates back to the early seventeen hundreds and is probably from England. I told you he was well known for his expertise in antiques."

"Yes, you did. I'm going to wash up, then we'll go downstairs."

"Okay."

We took a few minutes to get settled in before we went back to the study. When we entered the study, we could see that a table had been set for lunch. Along with the place settings, there was a silver tray with sandwiches on it.

Mr. Cox was sitting in a chair next to the window. He looked like a man with a lot on his mind. From what I knew from our previous phone conversation, he was hoping we would be able to find his son. He even may have been hoping that we would find his son alive, though I had some doubts. I was hoping we could find his son, too, but it was going to be tough.

He must have heard us enter the room as he turned around and smiled. He stood up and pointed toward the table. We joined him.

"Please, help yourselves," he said with a smile. "Since this is a working lunch, I'm ready to find out how much this is going to cost me."

We spent the next forty-five minutes or so explaining our fees and the amount of a retainer we wanted while enjoying some very delicious sandwiches. We also discussed the time and expenses that we had already spent on his behalf. He had no problem with what we had told him, and wrote out a check for the amount of the retainer requested, plus reimbursement for expenses we had already incurred.

As soon as we had finished our lunch and concluded our business, he showed us to the room where he had all the papers, reports from his previous investigators and from the police, as well as all the evidence he had been able to gather. It looked like a mountain of information. With so much information, I couldn't help but wonder why no one had been able to find his son. I also wondered what clues would be waiting for us to find among all the paperwork. It crossed my mind that we were being buried in paper like some lawyers like to do in an effort to bury the truth.

"This is everything I have on the case. I don't pretend to know how you do what you do, but if there is anything you need, just ask. Feel free to question any of my staff that you wish. If any refuse to answer any of your questions, let me know. So unless you have need of me, I will leave you to do what it is you do. I will call you when it is time for dinner."

"Thank you. Right now I don't have any questions of you, but once we have had a chance to start looking at these reports I'm sure we will," I said.

"Good. I will be available for the rest of the day should you wish to talk to me. But for now, I'll get out of your way," he said with a smile.

I watched him as he turned and left the room. As soon as he was gone, I turned and looked at Monica. She was looking at all the papers that were neatly stacked on the table as if it was overwhelming to her. She turned and looked at me.

I looked a little closer at the table. The papers seemed to have been in chronological order with the last dates first. They were also piled in stacks by the name of the investigators, with one pile that was police reports.

"I think I'll start with the police reports. Why don't you start by going through the reports of the first private investigator that Neil hired?"

"Okay, but what am I looking for?" Monica asked.

"You're looking for clues. You'll have no problem finding the big, important clues. They will stand out. It's the little subtle clues that are hard to find and often turn out to be the most important. Your studies in ancient artifacts should help you. When you find something that just doesn't seem right or seems slightly out of place, dig into it and find out what it really means. It's the same thing you would do with an artifact that doesn't seem to be what it looks like."

"Not really. With an artifact, I usually have it right in front of me," Monica said.

"Think of the reports as artifacts and look for what is there that doesn't seem right, or doesn't make sense, or what isn't there that should be."

"Okay, but don't expect too much. There's a big difference between police work and Archeology."

"Actually, there isn't that much difference. We are both looking for clues to what really happened at a given point in time and at a given place. The only difference is that in police work there are often people still living that can tell us what happened."

"I guess I never thought of it that way."

"Neither did I until now," I said with a grin. "Let's see what we can find before dinner."

Monica smiled at me, then picked up a small stack of papers and began looking through them. I picked up the stack of police reports, found a comfortable chair and sat down.

I started going through the reports. I took each report, one at a time, and read it carefully. The first report was of when Neil first reported his son was missing. It gave little information other than a complete description of what William looked like, what he was wearing when last seen, and the date and time that he was last seen by his father, Neil.

The following reports were follow-ups to the initial missing person report. Each one showed that the police had not found any leads that would help them find William. There were reports by officers who had followed up leads, but all seemed to come to an abrupt end.

The police had talked to everyone Neil had listed as someone William knew. Most of them appeared to be his friends. None of them stood out except for one that apparently had spent a good deal of time with William and was probably his closest friend. His name was James

MacPherson. From the address listed on the report, Mr. MacPherson lived just down the road.

It looked as if James MacPherson might be William's best friend, or at least one of his close friends. There was no doubt that MacPherson would be someone we should talk to in person about William.

The police report indicated that the local police had talked to James MacPherson more than once, but only once by Detective Longmont. I wondered why. There was nothing in the report to indicate why the detective had talked to him only once. I got the feeling that the local officer who talked to him believed he might know something he had failed to tell them. I thought the local officer might have been onto something. I had no idea what would come of it, but it was definitely a lead I should followed up on. It was a slim lead, but a lead none the less. I took a second to write down the name of the local officer on a legal pad along with his address.

On a separate piece of paper I wrote down the names of the others that the police had interviewed. I would follow up on those as well, but they didn't seem to be as important. They were local people who probably knew William.

Just as I was about to start going over another report, Koato came into the room and announced that dinner was ready in the dining room. I took a quick glance at my watch and realized that we had been at it longer than I thought. I stood up and walked across the room to Monica. She put the report she was looking at down and stood up.

"Did you find anything?" she asked as we followed Koato out of the room.

"I've found one person I would like to talk to. It looks like he might have been a close friend of William. Did you find anything?"

"Not anything I can say is a clue to William's disappearance."

"Remember, at this point even a little clue can be important," I said as we walked into the dining room.

* * * *

The room was very large with a dining table that looked like it was the size of a battleship. The only time I had seen a table like it was in the movies. It was set with places for four all at one end of it. Neil was standing at one end of the table waiting for us. Since I didn't see anyone else, I figured the fourth place setting was for his wife.

"Welcome," Neil said. "Please sit down. It will be just a minute before my wife will join us."

Monica and I walked over to the table and stood behind the chairs that Neil had directed us to. It was at that moment a door at the end of the room opened. A very frail looking woman in a wheelchair was brought into the room by Koato.

"Mia, I would like you to meet our guests. This is Nick McCord and his charming wife, Monica."

"Very nice to meet you," she replied with a very pleasant smile.

"It is nice to meet you, too," Monica said.

"Nice to meet you," I said.

"Shall we be seated," Neil said.

Koato pushed the wheelchair up to the table. Until then I had not noticed there was a place set at the table with no chair. I held a chair for Monica, then sat down beside her.

Once we were all seated, a nice looking older woman came in from the kitchen pushing a cart with silver serving bowls and covered platters on it. She took the lids off and placed the bowls and platters on the table. It was a meal fit for a king, and it was served as if Neil was the king.

"This is a very lovely home you have," Monica said to Mia.

"Thank you. It is a little large for our needs, but we do love it. It gives Neil room to store his antiques which he so dearly loves."

"The room we are staying in is absolutely beautiful," Monica said.

"I see that you also appreciate fine antiques. You must have Neil show you around. He knows the history of every single piece in this house."

"Thank you, I will," Monica said with a pleasant smile.

"I understand that you are here to see what you can do to find our son. Is that correct, Mr. McCord?"

"Yes, it is." I replied.

"What makes you think that you can do what several other investigators were unable to do?"

I looked at Neil, then at Monica before I turned and looked at Mia.

"Frankly, I'm not sure we can. At this point, all we are doing is looking at all the reports and evidence to see if there were any leads that had not been followed up, or any evidence that seemed to have been overlooked."

"And what will you do if you find any?"

"We will follow them up and see if they lead us anywhere."

"My husband tells me that you are the best in the business of finding people."

"I don't know if we are the best, but I would like to think that we are very good at what we do."

"It sounds like you are a confident person," she said with smile. "I like that in a person."

"Thank you," I replied.

"Nick, have you found anything helpful so far?" Neil asked.

"I'm not sure. I have found one person I would like to talk to."

"Who might that be?" Mia asked.

"James MacPherson. I believe he was a close friend of your son."

"James was William's best friend for many years. They were practically inseparable," Mia said with a note of sadness in her voice.

"I noticed that his address was just down the street a little ways. Does he still live there?"

"No. He lives in New York City. I have his address," Mia said.

"I would like to have it, please. Did he have any other close friends who might have had contact with William over, say the year before he disappeared?"

"I'm not sure, but I do have his address book," Mia said. "Would that be of any help?"

"It certainly could be of help."

"I'll get it for you after dinner.

"Thank you."

Dinner settled down into some small talk between bites. Mrs. Cox seemed to be very interested in Monica and her background as a History Professor at the University of Wisconsin and her expertise in antique jewelry. It was nice they seemed to get along well. Mr. Cox also seemed to want to know more about my past experiences as a police detective and some of the other cases I had worked on as a private investigator.

When dinner was over, we thanked them for the excellent meal and excused ourselves. We returned to the room Neil had provided for us. We hadn't been working very long when Koato came into the room and handed me William's address book. I thanked him for it and set it down. I would look it over later.

We continued to go over the reports until it was close to eleven o'clock. We decided that it was time to call it a night and went to the bedroom. It didn't take us long before we were in bed. I must admit that the large four poster bed was very comfortable. I laid there with Monica at my side thinking about what I had seen in the reports.

"What's on the agenda for tomorrow?" Monica asked.

"I was thinking we might start out by going into New York City and having a talk with James MacPherson. I would like to see where it takes us. I would also like to meet with Detective Marcus Longmont again."

"Why him?"

"I have a few questions I would like to ask him. I also would like to see the arrest records and the background checks on William. It just might get us pointed in the right direction."

"What direction is that?" Monica asked.

"At this point, I honestly don't know. Right now, I'm looking for something, anything that might help us find William. So far, I've only seen a couple of things that I would have done differently if I had been the cop looking for William. I have no idea if the results would be any different, but we would not be giving Neil his monies worth if we don't at least check it out."

"What would you have done differently?"

"I would have interviewed Susan Small, William's girlfriend," I said.

"Wasn't that the name of the cocktail waitress at Knollwood's?"

"Yes," I said. "I don't think Longmont spent very much time looking for her. I would like to know why he didn't take more of an interest in her. The report indicates his interview was with her parents, and that he never actually talked to her. I would like to know if he actually talked to the girl, and if he didn't, why. Also, if he didn't, I want to talk to her.

"I see your point," Monica said. "I didn't see any place where any of the investigators even knew he had a girlfriend, but I'm not finished going through all of them."

"She was just briefly mentioned in one of the earlier missing person reports. Nothing else is said about her," I said.

"Right now, I think we need to get some sleep. It could prove to be a long day tomorrow."

"You're right," I said. "What I need right now is a goodnight kiss."

Monica rolled over to me. I put my arms around her and pulled her close to me. Our lips met in a warm and passionate kiss. After several goodnight kisses, Monica rolled against me, closed her eyes and went to sleep. I watched her sleep for several minutes before I drifted off to sleep.

CHAPTER FIVE

I got up early the next morning, went over to the window and sat down on the window bench to think. The guestroom window looked out over the front drive and the neatly manicured lawn all the way to the road. I noticed a black Lincoln Town Car parked out front with a chauffeur standing near the backdoor of the car. The chauffeur was the same man that I had seen standing next to Neil when we arrived. He was obviously Neil's chauffeur and bodyguard.

I knew Neil was planning to go into New York City for the day. There was little doubt that he would have a chauffeur drive him so he could work on his way into the city. Neil was not the kind of man to waste a minute of time. He was the epitome of the old saying "time is money".

Just as I was about to leave the window and get ready to face the day, I saw Neil come out of the house. He was dressed in a dark colored business suit with a coordinated tie, and carried a briefcase. There was nothing out of place. He looked like the successful businessman that he apparently was.

The chauffer opened the backdoor of the car so Neil could get in. He then closed the door and walked around to the driver's side. I watched as the car left the estate. I wondered what kind of a business meeting Neil had in New York City. I knew he was an antique dealer and appraiser, but I had no idea if he was involved in any other business.

"What are you watching?" Monica asked from the bed.

"I was just watching Neil leave with his bodyguard," I said as I let the drapes fall back over the window.

"I guess we should get going, too, if we're going into the city."

"Yes. We're going," I said.

It didn't take us long to get dressed and get ready to go downstairs. As we came to the bottom of the stairs, we were met by Koato.

"Breakfast is ready when you are, sir. If you will follow me?"

"Thank you. I had noticed that our car was not out in front when I was looking out the upstairs window. We will need it for a trip into the city."

"I'll have it brought around for you, sir."

"Thank you."

After we had a delicious breakfast, we gathered up some of the information we thought we might need. We also packed an overnight bag in case we decided it would be necessary to stay overnight in the city, although it was not in our plans. We found the car parked out in front of the house when we were ready to leave. Koato was at the door to see us off.

"I can have a driver for you if you would like, sir," Koato said. "New York City is a little difficult to get around in if you are not familiar with it."

"Thanks for the offer, but I think we can find our way around."

"Very well, sir. Will you be back for dinner?"

"I'm not sure. Don't plan on us. We may not be back tonight at all."

"I see."

We got in the car and I drove down the long drive. I noticed that Koato stood at the front door of the house watching as we left. He was a strange little man, and I got the feeling that he knew a lot about the Cox family.

"Where to first," Monica asked, interrupting my thoughts.

"The Twelfth Precinct."

* * * *

It was not long before I was on the interstate that would take us into the city and to Manhattan. It took us over two hours to get to the precinct where Marcus Longmont worked. I found a parking place in the precinct parking lot that was designated for visitors. I parked the car, opened the door for Monica, then we went inside to talk to the desk sergeant on duty.

"Excuse me, sergeant, but I would like to know if Detective Longmont is in?"

"Yeah, he's here. Who are you?"

"I'm Nick McCord from Madison, Wisconsin. I talked to him the other evening. Would you please tell him that I'm here?"

The sergeant looked at me, then at Monica before he said, "Have a seat over there."

He pointed to a row of benches with high backs on them. There were only a couple of people sitting on them. I took Monica by the hand and led her to the benches.

"He sounds like he hasn't had his morning coffee, yet," Monica said with a smile as she sat down.

"I noticed, but I wouldn't be too hard on him. The desk sergeant's job is a tough one. He has to deal with all kinds of people all day long."

We sat quietly and waited. I didn't see the desk sergeant make any effort to call Detective Longmont for the better part of an hour. When he finally did contact him, he looked at us all the time he was on the phone.

"McCord," he called out as if he was a marine drill sergeant rather than a desk sergeant.

"Yes, Sergeant?"

"Longmont will see you now. Down the hall to the left, second door on the right," he said as he pointed down the hall we were to use.

"Thank you."

I took Monica by the arm and led her down the narrow hall to the second door on the right. I knocked on the door and waited for a response.

"Come in."

I opened the door and stepped into the office with Monica at my side. As soon as Longmont saw Monica, he stood up.

"Welcome," he said as he pointed to the chairs in front of his desk. "What brings you back here so soon?"

"We would like to talk to you about William Cox."

"I thought I covered that in the restaurant," Longmont said looking at me as if he wondered what I had on my mind.

"I'm sure you did, but I have a couple of questions for you."

"Shoot," Longmont said as he leaned back in his chair.

"I found in your interview reports that there was the mention of William having a girlfriend by the name of Susan Small. The thing is, I didn't find anything to indicate that you interviewed her. Did you interview her?"

"No."

I looked at him for a moment. It didn't seem to me that he was going to tell me anything more without a little prodding. It gave me the impression that he might be hiding something.

"Can you tell me why she wasn't interviewed?"

"Sure. She wasn't available."

"But you interviewed her parents."

"That's right. They were the ones who told me that she was unavailable."

"Did they tell you where she was?"

"Yes. They said she was in California at her grandparents place in, Santa Monica, I believe. I confirmed that she was there and had been for over a month before William disappeared."

"Did she ever return to New York City?"

"Not that I'm aware of."

"Did you make any attempt to find out if she had returned?"

"No. I couldn't see any reason to since she wasn't around at the time of his disappearance. It was a missing person case," he said with a hint of sarcasm.

"I see. I also noticed in your report that the local police interviewed James MacPherson on more than one occasion, but you interviewed him only once. Is that correct?"

"Yes."

"I got the impression from what you put in the report you filed that you didn't think he was telling you the complete truth, yet, you didn't interview him again. Can you tell me why you didn't go back and interview him again?" I asked as politely as possible.

"Yeah. I went to talk to him again, but I was greeted by his attorney. He was not too polite, I might add."

"I see."

"I still think he knew more than he was willing to tell me, but I didn't have grounds to bring him in and interrogate him. I had no proof that he was involved in William's disappearance or in anything unlawful. Talking to him wasn't going to produce anything usable as long as his attorney was present. If you want to have a talk with him, I'll get his address for you. Maybe you'll have better luck than I did."

"Thanks, but I have his address, and I do plan to talk to him."

"Good luck. Is there anything else I can help you with?" Longmont asked, but the tone and his appearance indicated that he really didn't want to hear from us again.

"Not right now."

"Let me know if I can help. As far as I'm concerned the case is still open."

"Thanks," I said as I stood up.

Monica stood up and took my hand. We left Longmont's office. She didn't say a word until we were in the car and ready to leave the parking lot.

"I thought you were going to ask him for William's arrest record. Why didn't you?"

"Did you notice that he was a little reluctant to answer my questions?"

"Yes."

"I doubt very seriously that I would have gotten a complete copy of William's police record. Someone is intentionally making it hard for us to find William. I got the impression that he was not very willing to share what he knows. He seems to be using the excuse that the case is still open. You use that excuse if you don't want to share information about someone."

"Is his police record important?" Monica asked.

"I won't know until I see it."

"How will you get it?"

"I'll have to call Frank Wallace again and have him get it. I'll have him send it to us at the Cox Estate."

"What's next?"

"I want to see if we can find James MacPherson. His address is in the file."

Monica picked up the file off the seat and began looking through it. She found the address we had and told me what it was. It took me a little over a half an hour to find it, and another twenty minutes to find a parking place.

Once I had the car parked, we got out and started walking. We had ended up almost a block from the front door to the apartment building where MacPherson was supposed to live. We were at the corner of the block, but on the opposite side of the street. We crossed the street after waiting for the light to change for us.

When we got to the address, we found ourselves in front of an upscale apartment building with a uniformed doorman.

I ignored the doorman as I turned and walked past him, but he stopped us just as I was reaching for the door.

"Can I help you folks?" the doorman asked rather sharply.

"No," I said. "We know where we're going."

"I'm sorry, sir, but I can't let you in unless I know who you are going to see."

"I'm going to see James MacPherson."

"Mr. MacPherson is not in at the moment."

"Are you sure?" I asked as if I was surprised to hear it.

"Yes, sir. He left for his office less than an hour ago."

"That's strange. It was my understanding that he was to meet us here," I said as I looked at Monica with a surprised look on my face.

"He didn't say anything to me that he was expecting guests. He must have forgotten. His office is only a couple of blocks from here."

I looked at Monica as if to see what she wanted to do. She is one smart woman. She caught on to what I was doing.

"Maybe he just forgot we were coming today, dear," she said.

"I suppose you're right, but I sure hate to come this far and miss seeing him," I said trying to look disappointed.

"I hate to disturb James at work, but then I hate to miss seeing him, too. Maybe this nice gentleman would be so kind as to tell us where his office is," she said with a beautiful smile that would disarm almost anyone.

"Certainly, Ma'am. You go down this way," he said as he pointed down the street.

After he finished giving us directions to MacPherson's office, we thanked him and started down the street.

We soon found ourselves in front of a high-rise building with fancy brass and glass doors. The sign on the door indicated that it was an insurance company. We walked into the lobby and looked around. The floor was brightly polished marble. On one side of the lobby was an information counter while on the other side was a bank of elevators. The information counter seemed to be our best choice at the moment since the building was so large. We walked over to the counter where a man in his mid-forties dressed in a suit greeted us.

"Good morning. How may I help you?" he asked with a pleasant smile.

"We've come a long ways to see Mr. James MacPherson. Could you tell us where his office is located?" I asked.

"Mr. MacPherson works in the claims section on the sixth floor. He is a claims representative and travels a good deal. However, he is in his office this week."

"Thank you."

"Take one of the elevators to the sixth floor and when you get off turn to the right. Go down the hall and you will see a sign above the door to the claims section. The lady at the desk will help you."

"Thank you."

We took the elevator to the sixth floor and turned right. There was a plastic sign above a door that read "Claims". We went inside and found a woman sitting behind a counter with a heavy glass window above it. We walked up to it.

"May I help you," she asked with a pleasant smile.

"We are Mr. and Mrs. McCord from Madison, Wisconsin. We are here to see Mr. MacPherson."

"Is he expecting you?"

"No, I don't think so."

"One moment please."

I watched her as she picked up the phone and called MacPherson's office. I couldn't hear what she was saying, but she looked at us as if she might not let us visit with him. She then hung up the phone and smiled at us.

"Mr. MacPherson said he didn't have an appointment with you. However, since you have come so far and he has a few minutes before he has to leave for a meeting, he will see you."

"Thank you so much," I said.

She buzzed us in then led us down a long hall. About halfway down the hall, she stopped at a door and knocked lightly before opening it. We entered the room while she retuned to her desk.

MacPherson was standing behind his desk when we walked in. He looked like he was about thirty years old, which would have been about the age William would be now. We knew that he and William had gone to school together, so that seemed to fit. He was wearing a rather expensive business suit with a very conservative silk tie.

"Welcome, Mr. and Mrs. McCord. Please have a seat," he said as he pointed toward the chairs in front of his desk. "What is it I can do for you?"

I had a feeling that when he found out why we were there, the silly grin on his face would disappear.

"First of all, you can tell us what you know about your friend, William Cox's disappearance."

I was right. The grin disappeared faster than ice melting on hot pavement.

"What is this about?"

"I thought I made that clear enough for you to understand."

"Who are you?" he asked, but his voice gave away the fact he was nervous.

"I'm Nick McCord and this is my wife. We are private investigators hired by Mr. Neil Cox to find out what happened to his son, William."

"I've told the police all I know."

"We happen to know that you told the police nothing. You let your lawyers do your talking."

"I'm not talking to anyone about it without my lawyer present."

"Interesting. Your best friend disappears, and you refuse to talk about it. That makes me wonder what you're hiding."

"I'm not hiding anything. I'm calling my attorney."

"Go right ahead, but let me warn you. If you don't talk to me, you will be talking to the police, again."

"Is that some kind of a threat?" he asked angrily.

"I realize you don't know me, so I'll explain something to you. I don't threaten people. Everything I say, I mean. By the way, I'll make sure that when they question you, it will be downtown, and they will remove you from your office in cuffs in front of everyone."

"You wouldn't dare."

"Are you willing to try me after what I just explained to you?" I said looking him right in the eyes.

MacPherson sat back in his chair and looked at me. I could tell he was thinking about it. It wasn't long before he took a deep breath, glanced at Monica, then looked at me again.

"What do you want to know?"

"When was the last time you saw William?"

"It was the night he disappeared."

"Tell me what happened that night. I might suggest you don't lie to me," I said.

Again, he took a long deep breath before he began talking.

"It was at my folks' house on Long Island. He had something to talk over with me."

"I take it he told you what it was he wanted to talk about?"

"Yes," he replied, but didn't say anything more.

"Well?"

"All he said was he needed money and he needed it fast."

"Did he tell you what he needed it for?"

"No, but from what I had heard he had been doing a lot of gambling. I figured he had gotten into some trouble over his gambling."

"So you knew about his gambling?"

"Yes."

"What was his attitude?"

"He was scared," James replied.

"Did you know about his drinking?"

"Yes, but I didn't think it was serious until that night."

"What caused you to change your mind?" I asked.

"He had been drinking."

"I understand that the two of you were pretty close. Is that correct?"

"We were until about five months before he disappeared."

"What happened to cause the change?"

"I'm not sure, but he began drinking and gambling. His father had to go bail him out of jail in Connecticut one night. As much as we were friends, I couldn't be associated with him. It could effect my position here," James said.

"You said you weren't sure what caused him to change. What do you think it might have been?"

"I can't say for sure, but it might have been a woman he met."

"Do you know who she was?"

"I don't know her name, but I think she lived in Connecticut."

"Why do you think she lived in Connecticut?"

"Because that was where he was always going," James said.

"Okay. Thanks for your help. I have just one other question. Why wouldn't you tell the police what you told us?"

"I don't know what William had gotten himself into; but whatever it was, I didn't want to get dragged into it. I had just started this job and didn't want any problems during my probation period."

"I see."

"You're not going to mention this to my boss, are you?"

"No. I have no reason to mention it to anyone. If I find out you lied to me, I will not keep quiet about it. I'll have you dragged out of here in cuffs to the police station."

"I didn't lie. I take it Mr. Cox is still trying to find out what happened to William?"

"That's right."

"I really hope you find him."

It was funny, but I got the feeling that he really meant that. However, I wasn't sure I should believe anything he said.

"If you think of anything else, it might be a good idea if you get in touch with me. This card has my cell phone number on it," I said as I stood up and handed him my card.

He stood up and took the card. Monica and I turned and left his office. She didn't say anything until we were out on the street.

"Do you believe him?" she asked.

"I'm not one hundred percent sure that he was telling us everything, but I think what he did tell us had some truth to it. I'm just not sure how much and what parts are true."

"You think he knows more than what he told us?"

"Maybe. I think I'll give our conversation with him some time to soak in and see if we find anything to support it. We may want to talk to him again."

"Where to now?" Monica asked.

"I'm not sure," I said as we walked back to the car.

CHAPTER SIX

Monica took my arm as we walked back toward where we had parked the car. We didn't talk much as we were wondering if we had really found out anything that would help. We did find out that William had been worried about something, but we still didn't know what. If we could find out what it was, we might be able to find out what happened to him.

When we got back to the car, we got in and just sat there. I wasn't sure what our next move should be. My thoughts were disturbed by Monica.

"Nick, look," she said as she pointed out the windshield.

I looked where she was pointing and saw James MacPherson. He was walking toward his apartment building and seemed to be in a bit of a hurry. I also noticed that he kept turning and looking behind him as if he was afraid that someone might be following him. He turned and went into his apartment building. I had seen the look on his face as he turned to go in. Although I was not very close to him, he looked scared. I wondered why. What was he afraid of? What had we said that made him so afraid he would leave work in the middle of the morning?

"I wonder what he's up to," I said more to myself than to Monica.

"I don't know, but whatever it is he looks like he's scared to death."

"I agree. I think we should wait and see what happens next."

"You think he might be planning to run?" Monica asked.

"Maybe, but what is he running from?"

Monica didn't answer. She sat quietly beside me and watched the front of the building. It was almost twenty minutes before anything happened. James came out of the apartment building with a suitcase in one hand and a smaller overnight bag in the other. He set them down next to the doorway and stayed close to the building while he looked around.

After talking briefly to the doorman, the doorman stepped out into the street and flagged down a cab. When the doorman opened the cab door, James looked around before he grabbed up his luggage and hurried to the cab. He didn't wait for the cabby to get out of the cab and put his luggage in the trunk. He shoved his luggage inside on the seat then quickly climbed in and closed the door.

"Get a cab number," I said to Monica as I started the car.

"I got it," she said just as the cab moved on by us.

As soon as it was clear enough and the cab was far enough away from us, I made a quick U-turn and hurried to get in position to follow the cab.

"Keep an eye on the cab," I told Monica. "I don't want to lose him."

I followed the cab through the mid-afternoon downtown traffic. It was not hard for me to stay a safe distance without him seeing us. Not knowing New York City very well, I wasn't sure where he was going.

Suddenly a delivery truck pulled out of an alley in front of us then stopped. I had no choice but to stop and watch the cab go on down the street. By the time I was able to get around the truck, the cab was gone.

"Did you see where he went?" I asked Monica.

"No. I think it turned right at the next corner, but I'm not sure."

"Damn."

I drove to the corner and turned. I looked down the street, but there was no sign of the cab. We had lost him. I needed to think. I pulled over to the curb and stopped. It was a no parking space, but I needed to think and I couldn't do it very well in all the traffic.

I sat behind the wheel trying to think about what we could have said that would make MacPherson run. I couldn't think of a single thing. It was possible that he had gotten a phone call just after we left and it had frightened him, but I didn't think that was it. I was reasonably sure that we had not frightened him enough to run, but something had. It could have been the fact we were looking for William, and we got him to talk.

I turned and looked at Monica. She had a disappointed look on her face.

"I'm sorry," she said looking at me.

"It's okay. It wasn't your fault. It's hard following someone in heavy traffic. At least we have the cab number."

"What good will that do?"

"I might be able to find out where the cab dropped him off."

"Will the cab company give you that information?" Monica asked.

"Probably not," I said with a sigh of disappointment.

"Do you have any idea where he might be going?" she asked.

"No, but I don't think he intends to come back soon. Since he didn't take a car, he is probably going to the train station to take a train back to Long Island where he can get his car."

"What do you want to do now?"

"I think we'll return to the Cox Estate and look over the reports some more. We might get lucky and find something that might help."

"Do you think William is still alive?" Monica asked.

"I don't know, but after this much time it's hard to believe he's alive."

Just then a police car pulled up behind us. I could see the officers getting out of their car in my rearview mirror. One was coming up beside me while the other was moving along Monica's side of the car toward the door. I looked at Monica.

"We've got company."

I rolled down my window and looked up at the officer as he walked up alongside the car. I knew I was illegally parked and about to get a ticket.

"You have a problem, sir?" the officer asked.

"No, sir. We're from out of town and got lost. We were just trying to get our directions."

"Do I know you?" the officer asked as he looked at me.

"I don't believe so. Like I said, we're from out of town."

"Where are you from?"

"Wisconsin. Madison, Wisconsin."

"Now I know who you are. You're Detective Nick McCord with the Milwaukee Police Department. You taught a class a few years back on preserving evidence at the scene of a crime. I was lucky enough to be able to attend the class. It's been a great help."

"Thank you. I'm not with the police department any more. I'm a private investigator now."

"You left the force?"

"Yeah."

"I'll be damned. Oh, excuse me, ma'am," he said as he glanced at Monica.

Monica just smiled at him.

"Can I help you find something?"

"No. I think we know how to get where were going, but thanks for your concern."

"Okay. You be careful out there. It was good to see you again."

"You take care, too," I said.

He reached up and touched the brim of his hat as he looked at Monica. I put the car in gear and pulled away from the curb. I glanced in the rearview mirror and could see the officer talking to his partner. It was one time when I was glad I was remembered.

I glanced over at Monica. She was looking at me and smiling.

"What?"

"I can't get over how many people you know all over the country."

"There are some who know me because of the class I taught, but I don't remember but a few of them. I'm glad the officer remembered me, otherwise we might have gotten a ticket for parking in a no parking zone. Tickets in New York City are not cheap."

Monica reached over and put her hand on my knee as I headed back out to Long Island. As I drove, my mind returned to thoughts of MacPherson. As I thought about him, I remembered his parents lived just down the road from Neil Cox.

"I think we should stop and visit with the MacPhersons before we return to the Cox Estate. What do you think?" I asked.

"I don't know. We have nothing to indicate that they would know anything," Monica replied. "But it sure wouldn't hurt any. We might find out where James was going in such a hurry. He may have returned to his folks' home. What better place to hide."

"I was thinking the same thing. If he went to the train station, he could have caught a commuter train out to Long Island. It wouldn't take him long to get home that way," I said.

Nothing more was said as I drove toward Long Island. It was a nice drive; and with Monica beside me, it was that much nicer. On our way back to the Cox Estate, we found a nice little seaside restaurant and stopped in for lunch. The food was good and the atmosphere was very pleasant. We discussed what we were going to talk to the MacPhersons about before we continued.

* * * *

We drove by the entrance to the Cox Estate and turned into the drive of the MacPherson Estate. There was no gate. We followed the long circular drive to the house. The house was not as large as the Neil Cox house, but it was still a very big house. It had a large porch with big white pillars. It looked typical of many of the large southern plantation houses in the south. When I thought about it, it seemed a little out of place in a part of the country where most old houses were Colonial style homes.

I stopped in front of the house and got out. A woman in a very nice Navy blue pants suit with white piping around the neck came out on the porch as I opened the door for Monica. As we walked up onto the porch, I could see that the woman was probably in her mid-to-late fifties. She stood very straight and tall, and her makeup and hair style were very fashionable for a woman of means. There was little doubt in my mind that she was the woman of the house.

"Good afternoon," I said with a smile.

"Good afternoon," she replied with a look of concern.

"My name is Nick McCord and this is my wife, Monica."

"I'm Mrs. Jeffery MacPherson. What is it you want?"

I got the impression she had been sent out to greet us by someone in the house. I had no proof, but I found it interesting that a woman who lived in this area would meet someone on the porch. It was more likely she would have had a servant answer the door. Someone had probably told her to expect us, and they didn't want us to see them. If that was the case, there was no need for us to hide the reason we were there.

"We have been hired to look into the disappearance of William Cox by Mr. Neil Cox. We would like to talk to you for a few minutes, if you don't mind."

"I've already talked to the police and several private investigators about William. I don't see that there is anything I could add at this late date," she said with a hint of sharpness in her voice.

"We have a few questions I hope will shed some light on his disappearance."

"All right. Please, come in."

She turned and went back into the house. Monica and I followed her to a small room just off the entryway.

"Please have a seat," she said as she sat down on a loveseat that looked to be very old.

"Thank you," I said as Monica and I sat down on a matching loveseat.

"What is it you think I can do for you?"

"William had talked to your son before he disappeared. We understand he talked to your son here, at your home. Is that correct?"

"I wouldn't know. My husband and I were in the city at a play. We stayed overnight at the Ritz. If my son said he was here, then I would think he was here."

"I believe that your son and William were pretty close."

"Yes, they were."

"What can you tell me about William?"

"Well, he was a very nice young man. Always polite, never rowdy. As an adult, he was always pleasant to be around. That is until the last few months before he disappeared."

"How did he change?" I asked.

"He seemed depressed. Nothing seemed to make him happy, and he had always been a happy young man and full of life. He had become moody and began to drink a lot."

"Did this effect James relationship with him?"

"Not at first. James tried to find out what was causing the change; but when William wouldn't talk to him about it, they drifted apart. When William started getting into trouble, James started to stay away from him."

"Do you know if James kept in touch with William?" I asked.

"I believe he did right up until William disappeared, but he didn't spend very much time with him."

"Do you think William would stay in contact with James if he could?"

"I'm not sure. He might. After all, they had been very close friends since they were small children," Mrs. MacPherson said thoughtfully. "Yes. I would think that they would stay in touch if it was possible."

"I want to thank you for your time, Mrs. MacPherson. I'm sorry we bothered you," I said.

"Does James have a girl friend?" Monica asked.

"No, I don't think so. You see, James is out of town a lot with his job."

"Thank you," Monica said.

"I hope I was helpful. Mia, Mrs. Cox, has been depressed ever since William disappeared. It would be a great help, and relief, to her if she only knew what had happened to her son even if he is found to have died. She needs to know what happened to him. I hope you can find something out if for no other reason than to give her closure."

"We will do our best," Monica said with a smile. "And thank you for talking to us."

"You are welcome."

"If you should think of anything that might help, please let us know," I said as I stood up. "We are currently staying with Mr. and Mrs. Cox."

"I don't know what else I could offer, but I will keep it in mind," she said as she stood up.

Monica and I turned and left the house. We walked down the steps of the porch to our car. I opened the door for Monica and waited for her to get in. Then I went around to the other side to get in. As I was opening the door, I glanced up at the house. I could see someone in one of the second floor windows. The drapes closed quickly as if whoever it was didn't want to be seen. I got in the car and started it, then drove down the drive.

"There was someone on the second floor watching us leave," I said as I turned out onto the road.

"Do you know who it was?"

"No, but if I had to guess, it was James."

"What makes you think that?"

"Whoever it was, he didn't want me to see him. As soon as he saw me look up at the house, he quickly closed the drapes."

"Could you tell if it was a man or a woman?" Monica asked.

"It was a man, but I'm not sure who."

"Then it could have been Mr. MacPherson, James's father?"

"It could have, but why would he not want me to see him?"

"Good question," she said, then sat quietly while I drove on to the Cox Estate.

CHAPTER SEVEN

I drove up to the gate at the Cox Estate and stopped so the guard could see us. He smiled, then immediately opened the gate so I could drive on up to the house. As I pulled to a stop in front of the house, Koato stepped out on the porch to greet us. As I was getting out, he opened the door for Monica.

"How was your trip into the city?" he asked Monica.

"It was pleasant," she replied, but offered no other information.

"Will you be here for dinner? I should let Mrs. Cox and the cook know you are back and will be having dinner here."

"Yes. I believe we will," Monica said. "Will Mrs. Cox be joining us for dinner?"

"I'm sure she will since Mr. Cox called and said that his meeting would probably run into the evening and he would be staying in the city tonight."

"Does he often stay in the city?" I asked.

"Not so much since William disappeared," Koato said.

"Where does Mr. Cox stay when he is in the city?"

"He has an apartment in his building."

"Thank you."

"I will tell Mrs. Cox that you have returned. She will be glad to know you will be having dinner with her," he said with a smile, then he picked up our luggage and headed into the house.

"I wonder why Mrs. Cox is so interested in our return," Monica said as we entered the house.

"Maybe she gets lonely for company when Neil stays in the city."

"That's probably it. She might like to have a little company, someone to talk to," Monica said with a smile.

"She might like to have a woman to talk to for a change," I suggested as I headed for the room that had been set up for us.

Monica followed me into the room. I walked over to the table were the reports were stacked. I was about to begin going through them looking for a clue into James and William's relationship during the few months before he disappeared. My thoughts were interrupted by Monica.

"Do you think James was telling us the truth?"

"I doubt that very much of what he told us was true, but there might have been some truth to it. My best guess would be he told us just enough that it would appear to all be the truth."

"What do you mean?"

"Part of what he said was true, and part of it was not. The problem is that we are left with the job of finding out what part is true and what part is a lie. Once we figure that out, we may have an idea what's really going on. Just the fact he left the city so quickly after talking to us leads me to believe he is involved in William's disappearance in some way, or he knows what happened and is afraid to say anything."

"I feel the same way, but what about Mrs. MacPherson? Do you think she knows more than she is telling us?"

"Maybe, but again I'm not sure. At this point, I don't have anything to corroborate either of their stories."

Monica didn't say anything after that, but I could tell she was thinking about it. Since I didn't think she had anything more to say at the moment, I began looking over the reports for anything that had something to do with James and what James had reported to the police and the private investigators. I was looking for changes in his story from one investigator to another.

I took a minute to glance at Monica to see what she was doing. Although Monica was sitting in front of a pile of reports, she was looking off into space. I wondered what it was that had her so distracted.

"What are you thinking about?"

"I was thinking about Mia. She probably spends a lot of time in this big house with no one to talk to."

"She might like to have someone to talk to. Maybe this would be a good time to talk to her," I said.

"You're right. We could talk to her without Neil or anyone else to interfere," Monica said thoughtfully.

"I was thinking more along the lines of you talking to her. She seems to like you and was willing to talk to you at the dinner table last night. She might still be willing to talk to you now. Who knows what she might tell you if I'm not there to listen in."

"Good idea," Monica said with a smile. "I wonder where she is now."

"Koato could tell you."

"I'll ring for him," Monica said with a big smile.

"Good. I'll continue to see what I can find out about James MacPherson in these reports."

I returned to looking through the reports. It was only a matter of moments before Koato came into the room.

"May I help you?" he asked.

"Yes," Monica replied. "Where would I find Mrs. Cox at this time of day?"

"I believe she is in the garden. Would you like me to tell her that you would like to visit with her?"

"No, I don't think so. I'm a little tired of all these reports. I think I would like to visit with her in the garden since it is such a nice day."

"Yes, Ma'am," he said. "Right this way."

Monica gave me a little wink as she followed Koato out of the room. I got the impression that Koato didn't like the idea of Monica talking to Mrs. Cox without Neil around. Was he afraid she might say something that Neil might not want us to know? I had confidence that Monica would be able to get any information from Mrs. Cox that she might know.

Since Koato was busy, I decided it was a good time to call Frank in Milwaukee for the police reports I had requested. I sat down at the desk by the phone and placed my call. The phone was answered quickly.

"Milwaukee Police Department, Fifth Precinct, how may I help you?"

"This is Nick."

"I've been waiting for you to call. I've got a lot to send you. It seems your boy has been a busy guy. I've got reports on him from New York City; Atlantic City, New Jersey; Ledyard, Connecticut; New Haven, Connecticut, and Hardwick, Massachusetts."

"Hardwick?"

"Yeah. It's a small town in north central Massachusetts. It seems he got pulled over there for speeding."

"How far back do these reports go?"

"About five or six months before he disappeared. There wasn't anything on file back any further and nothing after he disappeared. If he's alive, he's keeping a very low profile."

"Interesting. That's what we're finding," I said. "Can you do something else for me?"

"Sure."

"I'd like you to do the same thing for me on a James MacPherson. I don't know his middle name. He currently lives in Manhattan, but his folks live next to Cox on Long Island. I don't think he has lived in Manhattan very long. MacPherson was a close friend of William."

"I saw the name in one of the reports. I'm not sure which one, but I think it was the one from Hardwick."

"That's interesting," I said.

"I'll get started seeing what I can find out about this MacPherson guy. Give me your fax number and I'll get what I already have off to you."

I gave Frank the fax number and thanked him for his help. Almost as soon as I hung up I began to get the reports Frank told me that he was going to send. I began to put them in chronological order in the hope of getting some feel for what happened and the order in which it happened. I had no idea what it would show me, but it was the only thing I could think of at the moment. If I could get some idea of William's movements over the five or six months before he disappeared, I might be able to figure out what happened to him.

As the report from Hardwick came over the fax, I took a special interest in it. As soon as it cleared, I took it and began reading it. I found it interesting. It was dated the day before William was reported missing.

As I read the report, I realized that William had been stopped for speeding while he was going north. That would indicate he was going away from Long Island. I wondered where he was going. It also stated that James was a passenger, and he was the owner of the car William was driving. The report gave no indication that either of them had been drinking. It seemed safe to assume William had not been drinking at the time.

I tipped back in the chair and re-read the report. Based on what James had told us, I didn't like what I saw. James had said that the last time he saw William was at his parents' home the night he disappeared. The speeding report showed William was stopped late-afternoon, five forty-five to be correct, and he was headed north on highway 32A. James had also said that he was drunk. The speeding report gave no indication that either of them had been drinking. It was obvious James had lied to me. The only question was why?

I turned and looked out the window as I thought about what I had been told and what the report said. I quickly began looking for any report involving William after the stop by the Massachusetts State Police. The only ones I found that dealt with William were the missing person report and the reports of the search for William. There were no more reports indicating William had been seen after that stop, except for what James had told me.

The last official report I had of any direct contact with William was the one where he was headed north near Hardwick, Massachusetts. I wondered where he had been going. Did he ever get to his destination? Since James was in the car, and it was James's car they were in, the logical deduction was that James knew where William was going. James probably dropped William off somewhere, then returned to his parents' house.

I turned back around and looked at the police reports from Detective Longmont. I began going through them one at a time. Neil had indicated the police had not followed up on the case as they should have. I wanted to find out if he was right.

It was a slow, tedious job going over all of the reports. There were reports on Detective Longmont's interviews with Mr. and Mrs. Cox, with James MacPherson and the parents of Susan Small. I found the interviews didn't seem to have the depth that I would have expected from a police detective. It was almost as if Longmont was afraid to get into any kind of detail about William's disappearance and what he did in the months and weeks before he disappeared. In one of the reports was the statement by James MacPherson about having talked to William on the evening he had disappeared, and that William was drunk. My guess was James didn't think the stop by the state police in Massachusetts would ever be found out since it was out of state.

I again turned and looked at some of the other reports from private investigators. I wondered if they might have found more information. After all, they were not limited to jurisdictions. They could go anywhere they felt was necessary. I picked up the report from the first PI that Neil hired. His name was Bill Somersby.

Somersby lived in Stamford, Connecticut, just north of New York City. I knew there were several good PIs in New York City. I wondered why Neil had chosen one from Connecticut. It also caused me to wonder if Neil knew about Susan Small who lived in Avery Hills, Connecticut.

There was an address and phone number on the report. It would be a good idea to at least give Somersby a call and talk to him. I reached out and picked up the phone, dialed the number and waited for an answer.

"Somersby Investigations," a strong male voice said.

"Is this Mr. Bill Somersby?"

"Yes, it is."

"Mr. Somersby, my name is Nick McCord. I'm a private investigator from Wisconsin."

"What can I do for you, Mr. McCord?"

"I'm looking into the disappearance of William Cox. Do you happen to remember the case?"

"Sure. I'm not likely to forget it."

"Why is that?"

"I was hired to find William Cox by his father, Neil. I worked on it for almost six months and felt I was starting to get somewhere when Cox fired me."

"Why did he fire you if you were making headway on it?"

"I don't know," Somersby said. "Maybe he didn't think I was making enough progress on the case, but I got the feeling that he didn't want me to find his son. Why I felt that way, I'm not really sure. But I couldn't help feeling Mr. Cox was keeping something from me."

"I've been looking at your report. It seems that you were thinking he was hiding out somewhere, and believed he was not dead. Is that correct?"

"Sure. I had nothing to indicate he was dead or that anyone wanted him dead."

"What about his gambling?" I asked hoping he would provide some insight into it.

"What about it? He gambled and lost a lot of money, but as far as I could tell he didn't owe anyone anything. I didn't find any connections to gambling rings or loan sharks, or anything like that. He always had money and never spent more than what he had on him. I could find nothing to indicate he was into the mob for any amount of money, or that he was in debt to anyone."

"Then why did Cox want you off the case?" I asked.

"Like I said, I don't know?"

"What about his drinking?"

"Oh, he drank and drove drunk a few times, but I couldn't find anything to indicate it was a reason for him to just simply disappear. He wasn't what I would consider an alcoholic."

"What brought you to that conclusion?"

"He drank and gambled, but there were long periods of time he didn't drink. Most alcoholics I've met need to drink. And in most cases, need to drink everyday."

"Did you interview a Susan Small?"

"No," Somersby said. "She was supposed to be William's girlfriend. When I went to interview her, she had already gone to California, at least that is what I was told. In fact, I found out she had gone to California almost a month before William disappeared."

"Who told you about her being in California and when she left?"

"Her parents, actually it was the girl's mother who told me," he replied. "Her stepfather didn't say much."

"What are your feelings about this case?"

"Are you taking it on?"

"I might."

"Does that mean you haven't decided?"

"I'm still thinking about it. What I've found out so far makes me wonder what this is all about," I said.

"That was the feeling I had. There were a few things that just didn't add up, but I'm sure you already know that. As for me, I think William disappeared with James's help. I don't think he wants to be found. The reason, I have no idea. I do know his father, Neil, was pretty demanding of William. For some kids, that is reason enough to disappear," Somersby said.

"I'm sure you are right. I'm beginning to get the feeling that there is more to this than a simple disappearance."

"I agree with you, but I never got the time to figure it out."

"Thanks for your help," I said.

"If there's anything I can do for you, let me know," Somersby said.

"Will do."

"Oh, there's one other thing I think you might like to know," Somersby said. "When Cox terminated my employment with him, he paid me very well and made reference to our agreement of confidentiality. I got the feeling he was hiding something from me, but I was never able to figure out what it was."

"Thanks. I'll keep that in mind. By the way, our conversation will remain between us."

"Understood. Good luck," he said then the phone went dead.

I turned and looked out the window again. I wondered what was going on. There was no indication William was dead, but there was some suspicion that he was running from something. Somersby indicated it might be his father. I wondered if he was right.

I returned to the reports of the other PIs Neil had hired. I found nothing more than I had found in the first report. It seemed that every time an investigator was getting anywhere close to discovering something that looked like it might be important, or the investigator found something that looked like it could be a good lead; Cox fired them after paying them very well for their services. What was it that they were getting close to that Cox didn't want them to find? I could only hope to find a clue to what it was in amongst the reports in front of me.

It would take a lot of searching, but I was determined to find out what Cox was hiding. To get the answers I needed, I began by sitting back and reading each and every report very carefully. A long process, but the only thing I could think to do at the moment.

CHAPTER EIGHT

I was deeply involved in a report from a New Jersey PI when Monica came into the room. She was grinning from ear to ear. There was little doubt in my mind that she had found out something she felt was important to our case.

"Well, you look like you had a nice visit."

"I did. Mia is a very nice lady."

"What happened?" I asked, curious as to what they had talked about.

Monica walked up close to me and leaned toward my ear.

"I think we should take a little walk outside."

I leaned back and looked her in the eyes. It didn't take a degree in Criminal Justice to understand what was going on.

"I'm a little tired of being cooped up in here going over all these reports. How about we take a walk so I can stretch my legs?" I asked.

"That sounds like a great idea."

I took Monica by the hand and led her out the front door. We walked past the car that was still parked in front of the house then on across the drive to the lawn. As we stepped onto the well manicured lawn, she took my arm and leaned against me.

"Why all the secrecy?" I whispered.

"From the way Mia acted in the garden, I got the feeling that the room we are working in might be bugged."

"Okay. I get the feeling we will be taking more walks around here. How did things go with Mia?"

"Mia and I had a nice talk. She doesn't believe William is dead."

"She told you that?"

"It took awhile, but she indicated that she would not be surprised to find out that William has run away."

"Is that what she believes?"

"I don't know if she really believes it or not. It may be her way of not facing the possibility that William is dead," Monica said. "We spent a lot of time talking about William when he was a boy. She said he and his father had terrible arguments when he was a teenager."

"Did William ever run away from home?"

"I don't know. She never said he had, but I got the impression that he might have tried. She did say that after William turned eighteen, the two of them seemed to grow closer together. Neil started teaching William the business of antiques and how to appraise them."

"What do you make of it?" I asked. "Do you think it was just a phase William was going through?"

"It certainly could have been. I just don't know. After William graduated from high school, Neil bought him a fancy sports car and enrolled him in a school so he could learn to appraise antiques. During his time in school, William spent a good deal of the year away from home. The school was somewhere in Massachusetts, near Boston. It didn't sound as if he got home very often. Mia said he did very well at the school. She was so proud of him," Monica said.

"There was no record of William getting into any kind of trouble prior to the five or six months before his disappearance. What I would like to know is what happened to change him."

"I didn't get a hint of anything that would help us figure out what might have caused the change in him," Monica said. "However, she quit talking when I asked her if William finished the school and went to work for his father. She said that he finished school, then she seemed to not want to talk anymore. She said she was tired and called for Koato to take her to her room to rest."

"Do you think she was using it as an excuse to avoid talking about William?"

"It might have been. I'm hoping to get to talk to her again. I hope I didn't push her to hard," Monica said as she looked at me with a worried look on her face.

"I wouldn't worry about it. Leave her alone for a while. She may want to talk to you again later."

"Okay. There was one thing I noticed. When Koato came to take her to her room, I don't know, but the way she looked at him made me wonder," Monica said, but didn't continue.

"Made you wonder about what?" I asked.

"It seemed that she felt very close to Koato. Closer than one would expect."

"I would think she would be close to him. After all, he is here all the time with her and he takes care of her."

"I guess you're right," Monica said as she looked up at me.

I took a minute to look around as we continued our walk across the lawn. I was thinking about what Monica had said concerning what Mia had talked about. I had not been able to find anything in any of the reports that would lead me to believe William's disappearance was due to a bad relationship between him and his father. However, it was something I believed we should explore as a possibility.

The fact that William had gone to school to study antiques had not come up in any of the information I had, but it was beginning to look like it might be important.

"How did your afternoon go?" Monica asked disturbing my thoughts.

"Not too bad. I got hold of one of the first PIs Neil hired shortly after William had disappeared. I think he was doing a good job following leads based on his reports. He might have been getting close to figuring out what happened, but Neil fired him before he could figure it out. In talking with him, he confirmed what I felt his reports indicated."

"That doesn't make sense," Monica said.

"It does if Neil doesn't really want his son to be found."

"If he doesn't want his son to be found, then why is he going to all the trouble to make it look like he will never give up on looking for him?" Monica asked looking a bit confused.

"Maybe to hide something he doesn't want anyone to know?"

"That would certainly be a reason," Monica agreed.

"Let's head back to the house. We still have a lot of reports to read. Somewhere in all those reports is the answer. If not the answer, there is a clue that might lead us to the answer."

"I take it we are going to find out what happened to William regardless of what Neil really wants?"

"You got it," I said with a grin.

"I'm with you on this one. I want to know what happened to William even if Neil fires us."

"Good," I said as I drew her to my side and squeezed her gently.

I leaned over and gave Monica a gentle kiss on the cheek. She smiled as we turned and headed back to the house.

As we walked toward the house, I glanced up at the second story. I saw Koato in the window watching us. He quickly let the drape close over the window.

"I saw Koato watching us from a second story window."

"I'll bet he was upset that we took a walk to talk," Monica said as she looked up at me and smiled.

"You would probably win that bet."

As we entered the house, we found Koato standing in the entryway waiting for us. He smiled, but it was not a friendly smile.

"Is there anything I can get you?" he asked politely.

"I don't think so. We took a breather. I think we will return to the reports," I said.

"Very well, sir," he said as the turned to leave.

"Koato?"

"Yes, sir," he said as he turned back to look at us.

"I was wondering something. How long have you worked for Mr. Cox?"

"A little over thirty years, sir."

"Then you know Mr. Cox and his family pretty well."

"Yes, sir. Probably better then almost anyone," he said with an air of pride.

"How did Mr. Cox and William get along?"

I couldn't help but notice the slight change in the way he looked at me. He didn't seem to want to answer the question. I believed he needed a little coaxing.

"If you will remember, Mr. Cox said that I could ask any of the staff anything I wanted, and he had instructed members of his staff to answer our questions. This silence from you indicates you are not as willing to answer my questions as Mr. Cox had suggested. Is that so?"

"No, sir."

"Then you will answer my questions honestly?"

"Yes, sir. Mr. Cox and William had their problems when William was a young teenager, as do many parents. But William grew out of it and began to respect his father. They even began to work together. They were getting along very nicely."

"What happened to change that?"

"What do you mean?"

"You know what I mean. About five or six months before William disappeared, William changed. I want to know why?"

"I'm afraid I don't know what you are talking about."

"I see," I said as I stopped and simply looked at him for a moment. "You have no intentions of cooperating with us. Do you?"

Koato looked at me, but didn't answer. I could see that he was thinking about how much he should say.

"William and Mr. Cox had a falling out about five months before he disappeared."

"What was it about?"

"I don't really know, sir. All I know is that William started spending a lot of nights away from here. He came home drunk a couple of times. It didn't set well with Mr. Cox. One afternoon right after lunch, they had an argument in Mr. Cox's den. It got rather loud. During the argument Mr. Cox struck William. William stormed out of the house with his hand over his cheek."

"What was the fight about?"

"I have no idea. I couldn't hear what went on, but when Mr. Cox came out of his den he was mad as hell. Excuse me, sir."

"That's okay," I said with a slight smile.

It was the first time that Koato had let his guard down. The fight between William and Neil had obviously upset him.

"After Mr. Cox stormed out of the den, I made myself very scarce for the rest of the day."

"When did this happen?"

"It would have been the day before William disappeared."

"Did you see William anytime after the argument?"

"No, sir. It was the last time I saw him."

"Thank you. I will not say anything to Mr. Cox about our conversation. If I need to bring it up to him, I'll find a way not to involve you."

"Thank you, sir. I would like you to know that I liked William very much. I hope you can find out what happened to him."

I simply nodded then turned around. I took Monica by the hand, then led her back outside. We were well away from the house before she said anything.

"What do you make of that?"

"I'm not sure, but the argument had upset Koato a great deal. We need to take a look at some of the other reports. I want to see if we can find what's missing from the reports. I have serious doubts that the reports Neil gave us are complete. I would bet they have been carefully reviewed, and maybe revised, so there is nothing that will lead us to finding William or the reason he disappeared."

"So I'm to look for what is not there, rather than what is?"

"That about sums it up."

Monica looked at me as if I had lost it. The only thing I could think of was that she might be right.

"Nick, how do I do that?"

"Look for leads that were not followed up when the PI was terminated. That would indicate the PI was getting too close to solving it, or had a pretty good idea of where it was going. Make a note of the PI and where we might find him. We'll want to talk to him in person.

"Also look for reports that when you read them sound as if something is missing or it doesn't seem to make sense. Even look for the possibility that a page is missing from the report, or part of it has been rewritten."

Monica nodded that she understood. We returned to the house and began looking through the reports again. We had a couple of hours before it would be time for dinner.

CHAPTER NINE

Monica and I had spent the afternoon going over the reports from nine private investigators looking for some reason for Neil to have fired them. It may not lead us anywhere, but it was something that didn't seem right and had to be investigated to find out what it did mean. With the exception of four of them, the others looked like they were making some progress. They had leads to follow up on and had talked to what I thought were probably the right people. I could see no reason for Neil to have fired them.

The four that didn't seem to be getting anywhere and didn't seem to be following up on anything, looked to be second rate investigators who were just taking Neil's money and doing nothing to have earned it. At least that was the way it looked to me. From what I could see in the reports submitted by the four second rate investigators, it looked as if Neil kept them around longer than the others. Since it was so obvious, I wondered why.

Why would anyone keep a PI on the payroll when it was so obvious he was not producing any results? I could think of only one reason that seemed to make any sense, and that was to make it look like Neil was actually doing everything he could to find his son. The question that crossed my mind was who was he trying to impress? Who was he putting on this expensive show for in order to make it look like he was not giving up on finding his son when his actions told me he had given up a long time ago?

I could think of two people he might be putting on the charade for. The first, and most obvious, was his wife. It was apparently working. Mrs. Cox had told Monica that she was convinced William was still alive, although she couldn't provide any proof. Maybe it was just a mother's hopefulness.

The second was for Neil's clients. It might get him some degree of sympathy. It might also get him some support from friends and even clients as well as make him look like the perfect father who would not give up in the search for his only son. From the looks of the evidence, just the opposite was true.

There was a third possible reason that passed through my mind. It was to keep any suspicion of his son's disappearance from falling on him. We knew from Mia that Neil's relationship with his son had been rather strained at least during William's teenage years. I wondered if it might have continued into William's adulthood, although Mia had indicated that it had not. I wasn't sure how much of what Mia had told Monica was true, or how much had been fabricated by either Neil or Mia.

Then there was what Koato had told us. If what he told us was true, it didn't appear as if William and Neil were getting along very well right up to the time William disappeared. I wondered just how bad their relationship might have become. More importantly, what was the reason they didn't get along?

Although I had no proof of anything at this point, I was beginning to wonder if William might be dead. If he wasn't alive, I was beginning to think Neil might know what had happened to him. And if that was the case, there was a good possibility Neil already knew where William's body might be. The problem I had was in what I couldn't prove.

"Monica, I think it's time to take a short walk. I need to stretch my legs and get a little fresh air."

Monica looked over at me and smiled. She knew just what I was saying. I could tell by the look on her face that she was sure I had found something of importance.

"I think that's a good idea. My brain can't look at another report," she said.

As we left the room, we found Koato in the entryway. He had a look on his face that made me think he had been trying to listen in on what we had talked about. I smiled to myself because he would have been listening to nothing. For the past few hours, Monica and I had hardly spoken a word to each other. We had simply gone over the reports one by one and wrote down the names, addresses and phone numbers of the private investigators Neil had hired and fired.

I also knew that Koato wouldn't find anything of interest in the room after we left if he decided to take a look at what we were doing. I had picked up the lists of the PIs we were going to visit and any other notes we had made. I had folded them and put them in my pocket. I didn't want anything left in the room that would even hint at what we were planning to do.

Once we were outside and away from the house, Monica turned and looked at me. She was waiting for me to say something.

"Have you noticed that every single PI who was interviewing the right people and following up leads was fired when it looked like he might be making good solid progress?" I asked.

"Yes. I found that to be the case, but I'm not really sure what I was looking for to begin with. However, I saw in a couple of reports that it didn't seem as if PIs were doing anything. It was almost as if they were just taking Neil's money and not really earning it," Monica said.

"Neil also seemed to keep those PIs around longer."

"I noticed that, too. It doesn't make much sense," Monica said.

"I think it does if Neil is trying to hide something. I think it would be a good idea to start talking to the PIs that seemed to be making some headway. It could prove helpful to get their insight. It's not always what they know and can prove that helps. Sometimes it's what they think they know and can't prove."

"I think you're right. When do we start?" Monica asked.

"Tomorrow morning. We'll start with the out of state PIs. I already talked to one in Connecticut, but there's another out of Hartford. There's also one in New London."

"There's also one in Glastonbury," Monica said. "I remember seeing his reports."

"I wonder why Neil hired one out of Hartford," Monica said. "It seems like a long way away from here."

"I'm not sure, but I plan to ask the PI that very question."

"What are we going to use as an excuse for leaving?" Monica asked.

"I think we will tell Koato that we are going up to Knollwood's to have another talk with Bradford about William's gambling and drinking," I said.

"Maybe we should go back in. I caught a glimpse of Koato watching us from one of the second story windows. He sure seems interested in what we are doing."

"I would be willing to bet it is his job to keep an eye on us when Neil is not around."

Monica smiled, then said, "He's not very good at keeping an eye on us without us knowing about it."

I just smiled at her as we started back toward the house. It only took a few minutes for us to get back in the house. We were once again greeted by Koato when we entered.

"Dinner will be ready in just a few minutes," he said with a polite smile.

"Thank you," I said."

"You can go into the dining room now if you like. Mrs. Cox is waiting for you."

"Thank you," I replied.

I looked at Monica and she nodded. We turned and headed toward the dining room.

When we entered the dining room, we saw Mrs. Cox sitting at the end of the table where Mr. Cox had sat last night. She smiled when we came in.

"Please, come and sit down with me," she said as she spread her arms to indicate the places set for us.

I saw there were places set on either side of the table near the end. I followed Monica down the table and held a chair for her as she sat down. I then went around the end of the table and sat down across from Monica.

"How are you coming with your investigation? Are you finding anything of interest in all those reports?"

Monica looked at me as if she wasn't sure what she should say. I turned and looked at Mrs. Cox.

"I'm not sure, but I think we may have found a lead. It's nothing to get excited about at this time, but it does look promising."

"Can you tell me what it is?" she asked as her eyes sparkled.

I was a little surprised to see her in such good spirits tonight. The other night at dinner she appeared tired and weary. She hadn't talked much to either of us and kept glancing at Neil as if she was looking for direction from him. She had looked like someone who had been hoping for so long that it had drained her of all her energy.

However, tonight she looked much different. It was almost as if she was on top of the world or she was high on some drug, but there were no signs that she had been taking anything. The difference was unbelievable. Then again, maybe it was because Neil was not there to hear what she had to say.

"About all I can tell you at this point, is that we are going to be gone for a few days to talk to some people who may be able to help."

"Have you talked to James, James MacPherson?"

"Yes, we have. We also talked to Mrs. MacPherson."

"Did it help you any?" she asked.

"I'm sorry, but not as much as I had hoped," I said hoping that I had not caused her to lose hope. "We didn't get a chance to talk to Mr. MacPherson, however."

"Mr. MacPherson died about three years ago," Mia said. "She lives in that big house all alone since James moved to the city."

I looked at Monica. She was looking at me. She knew I had seen a man in a second story window.

"You know that James and William were very close friends?" Mia asked.

"Yes, we know that."

"You know that James saw William the afternoon before he disappeared?"

"Yes," I replied. "James told us."

I looked at Monica then looked at Mrs. Cox. I didn't tell her that there was a discrepancy in the stories we got from Mrs. MacPherson and James, and now from her.

"Did you see them together?" I asked.

"Yes."

"What did you see?"

"I saw the two to them leave from MacPherson's drive in James's car. William has a very nice car of his own. It is much nicer than James's car," she said proudly.

"About what time was that?"

"It was very shortly after noon, I'd say about – one o'clock," Mia said.

I had been leaning forward listening to her every word, but leaned back when dinner was brought in. I glanced at Monica while I waited for all of us to be served. As soon as the waiter left the room, I looked at Mrs. Cox again.

"Do you have any idea where William might have been going with James?"

"No. He never said a word about going anywhere that night, but then he didn't often tell me where he was going."

"Did you know that William went to Knollwood's Resort and Casino in Connecticut several times in the months before he disappeared?"

"I knew that James and William liked to go to Knollwood's and went on a number of occasions together. Yes."

It was the first time we had any indication that William had gone with anyone. James had certainly not said anything about going with him. Yet we knew he had been with William when he was ticketed for speeding near Hardwick, Massachusetts.

"Do you happen to have any idea why James and William would be going to Massachusetts?"

"The MacPhersons have a cabin in Massachusetts. It is somewhere around Athol, I believe. That's in the north-central Massachusetts."

"Have you ever been there?"

"No, but William has been there several times with the MacPhersons. They would take William with them sometimes in the summer when the boys were younger," Mia explained. "Why? Is that important?"

"I don't know. Hardwick was mentioned in one of the reports, is all."

"I don't know of any reason why William would have gone to Hardwick. We don't know anyone who lives there."

"Mrs. Cox, do you know where William's car is now?" I asked.

"Yes. It is in the carriage house where it has been for the past five years."

I don't know why, but I was a bit surprised that they had kept the car. I glanced at Monica. She looked at me as if to ask what I was going to do next.

"I've insisted it be kept for William when he comes back," she said as if reading my mind. "He loved that car more then anything."

"Would you mind if I take a look at it?" I asked. "There may be something that just might help us find William."

"Not at all, if you think it will help. Neil had it put in the old carriage house out behind the garage."

"Is that where he always kept it?"

"No. He used to keep it in the garage with our cars. After William didn't return for six months, Neil wanted to sell it. It was still in Neil's name so it would not have been a problem for him to sell the car. I asked Neil not to sell it, so he put it in the carriage house to get it out of the way. I think Neil had a hard time looking at it whenever he went to the garage."

At the moment, I didn't have any more questions to ask Mrs. Cox. Monica picked up the conversation during dinner. Monica talked to Mia about her garden and how she was getting along. It looked as if Monica and Mia were getting along pretty well. I was hoping Monica would be able to get close to her, and in that way find out more about the family and William.

"Would you like to come into the parlor for a cup of tea," Mrs. Cox asked after dinner was over.

"I would," Monica said with one of her disarming smiles.

"I would, too, but I think I would like to take a look at William's car. I will join you later, if you don't mind."

"I understand," Mrs. Cox said. "You will find the key to the carriage house in a metal box on the wall next to the backdoor. Through that door," she said as she pointed to the door to the kitchen.

"I'll join you ladies later," I said with a smile.

As I was leaving the dining room, I saw Monica pull Mrs. Cox's wheelchair away from the table, then turn her and push the wheelchair toward the parlor.

CHAPTER TEN

I found the key to the carriage house right where Mrs. Cox said it would be. There were also a number of other keys in the box. They were all clearly marked. There was even one marked "William's car". I took the key to the carriage house and the one to William's car. Then I went out the backdoor.

About fifty yards from the house was an old two story carriage house. On the upper level there was a large door where bales of hay would have been hoisted up to the door, pushed inside and then stacked in the upper level for use during the winter. The large carriage house door on the ground level had a smaller door cut in it so a person could enter the carriage house without opening the larger door.

After unlocking the small door, I opened it and stepped inside. The first thing I noticed was the center of the carriage house had a long, fairly wide aisle running down the center of it. There were several stalls for horses on both sides of the aisle. There were five stalls on one side and four on the other. The space where the fifth stall would have been was enclosed and was apparently used as a storage room, probably a tack room. Toward the far end of the center aisle was a car covered with a tarp. The tarp distorted the shape of the car so that I could not tell what kind of car it was from where I was standing.

It was dark enough inside the carriage house that it made it hard to see in the stalls and to make out what might be in them. Yet it was light enough that I could tell what was in the aisle. I looked around for a light switch and found it next to the door. The lights down the middle of the carriage house came on when I flipped the switch. I stood by the door and took a minute to look around. The floor in the carriage house was hard packed dirt.

As I moved down the center aisle, I noticed a couple of the stalls stood open. In one of them was an old fashion carriage typical of those used by wealthy people in the late nineteenth century and very early twentieth century. The carriage was covered with a layer of dust and cobwebs. Some of the leather was cracked and dry from a lack of care. It was obvious that it had not been used for a very long time. I was a little surprised to find it in such poor condition since Neil was an antique collector and would know the value of such things. There were no horses in the stalls, but I had not expected to find any.

I went on down the aisle to the car that was covered with a tarp. I pulled the tarp up and laid it back on the hood so that I could see the front of the car. It was a red Jaguar convertible, a Jaguar "E" type to be more accurate. It was a nineteen sixty-two classic in every sense of the word. The car had been given to William as a present for graduation from high school. It was probably a classic when he got it.

As I stood there looking at it, I noticed that there was a small dent in the left front fender and the bumper was bent slightly on the left side. It wasn't anything that couldn't be fixed in a good body shop. I wondered when it had happened and what had come in contact with the fender. It had probably been the result of one of William's trips where he damaged the car while driving drunk. A closer look at it revealed some paint scrapings that looked to be about the same color as the trim on the carriage house.

I decided it might be a good idea if I took a look at the entire car. I pulled the tarp off the car, then stepped back to look it over. I walked all the way around it. There was no other damage to the outside of the car. I did notice that the license plates had been removed from the car. If it had been parked there as a place to store it, why bother to remove the license plates? I would have not been surprised to see license plates that had been expired for five years. Without the license plates, I had no idea when the last time it had been registered. That tidbit of information just might prove interesting.

I zipped open the tonneau cover and unsnapped it so I could look inside the car. The car was clean on the inside except for a thin coat of dust. A search of the inside of the car provided nothing of interest except a small piece of paper with an address on it. I had no idea how much help it would be. It was only a road address with no mention of a city or state. There was also no way to tell how long the address had been in the car or who had left it there, since the car was a nineteen sixty-two, and William was not the original owner.

I stood back and looked at the car as if it was going to talk to me. Why had William gone off in James's car and not taken his own? Was it because the car would stand out? Was it because it would have to be licensed which would make it possible for someone to track him? I also wondered why Neil had moved the car to the carriage house. Was it hard for him to look at the car every day as Mia had suggested, or was there some other reason?

In order to get some idea of how long the car had actually been there, I put the key in the ignition and turned it. Nothing happened, which I fully expected. Either the battery was dead or it had been disconnected and probably removed. I opened the hood, or the front bonnet as the British would call it, and found the battery missing. If I was going to store a car for a long period of time, I would have removed the battery, too.

I decided to take a look in the glove box. I had no idea what I would find there, but to fail to look could mean I would miss something important. I found a map of Massachusetts, one of New York, one of Connecticut and one of New Jersey. There was also the registration for the car. I glanced at it, then started to close the glove box, when something about the registration caught my eye. I picked it up and held it to the light. The last date the registration had been renewed was almost six months after William had disappeared. If what I was told was true, then why was the registration renewed? I put the registration back in the glove box after writing down the date the registration had been renewed. I slipped the paper in my pocket. The registration left a lot of unanswered questions.

I opened the rear bonnet, or trunk, to see what might be there. Lying on the floor of the trunk were the license plates for the car. The sticker on the corner of the plates showed the licenses had been renewed after William had disappeared. I wondered why the license plates had been renewed if no one drove the car after William disappeared. The answer was simple, someone licensed it to drive it. Where had it been taken? And who had taken it?

Since there didn't seem to be anything else gained from the car, I closed the front and rear bonnets. It was time to cover it back up and leave it just the way I had found it. After closing the tonneau cover, I put the tarp back over the car making sure that I covered it like it had been.

I then stepped back and looked around the carriage house. The only places I had not looked were in the loft and the tack room, or at least what I thought was probably the tack room. I decided to start with the tack room.

I walked up to the tack room door and found it unlocked. I opened the door and stepped inside. It was dark in the room as there were no windows. I looked for a light switch and found one next to the door. I flipped the switch and the room filled with light from a single light bulb hanging from the ceiling in the center of the room. I had been right, it was a tack room. One wall was covered with harnesses and other leather straps such as reins. There were a couple of old saddles and bridles, too. A number of old tools such as racks, shovels and pitch forks that would have been used to keep the carriage house and stalls clean were leaning against the wall. I left the tack room and climbed the ladder to the loft. Once I was in the loft, I found several old bales of hay, but nothing else. It had turned out that the only thing of interest was the car, and that didn't provide very much information as far as I could tell at the moment. It was time to go back to the house and see if Monica had learned anything new from Mrs. Cox.

Just as I got back to the floor of the carriage house, Koato came in the small door. When he saw me, he quickly looked at the tarp covering the car.

"I – ah – I saw the light on and wondered who might be in here," he said.

"It's just me looking around."

"I don't think Mr. Cox would like you in here."

"Why's that? Mrs. Cox doesn't seem to have a problem with it."

"Mr. Cox doesn't like anyone in here."

I got the hint that he wasn't going to tell me why Neil didn't like anyone in the carriage house, but I had a feeling he knew why. There was little doubt in my mind he would tell Neil as soon as he could that I had taken the tarp off the car.

"Tell me, if this car was stored in here six months after William disappeared, and no one is supposed to have driven it, why was the license renewed almost six months after William disappeared?"

Koato looked at me for a moment or two before he responded.

"Mr. Cox licensed it so he could show it to someone who was interested in buying it."

"I was told that Mrs. Cox didn't want it to be sold."

"That's right. She found out Mr. Cox was going to try to sell the car. She demanded that he not sell it."

"I take it she got her way," I said.

"Yes, sir. She did get her way," he said with a slight grin.

I smiled at Koato. He seemed to like the idea that Mia had gotten her way.

"I'm ready to leave," I said as I walked by him toward the door. "How about getting the lights when you leave?"

"I will, sir," he said as he watched me walk back to the house.

When I got to the house, I found Monica waiting for me in the room Neil had setup for our use. She was sitting at one of the tables reading a report when I walked in. She turned and looked at me.

"Find anything interesting?"

"No." I said as I smiled at her.

Monica was a very smart woman. She knew from my smile I might have found something of interest, but I didn't want to say anything about it where there was a possibility it might be overheard.

"I think I've about had it here. I need to get away from all these reports for a little while. My brain can't take much more tonight," Monica said.

"What do you say we take a little walk before we go to bed?"

"Sounds like a good idea," Monica said as she got up and walked toward me.

We left the house and went for a walk along the drive toward the road. I held her hand as we walked.

"What did you find out?"

"Not much really," I said.

I began by telling her about the car in the carriage house. It was only when I told her about the address I had found in William's car that she looked surprised.

"You found an address in his car?"

"Yeah. It was on the floor between the seats."

"Any idea how it got there?"

"None. But I'm sure it had been there for a long time."

Monica didn't say anything, but she was thinking. About what, I wasn't sure.

"Do you think it might be the address of MacPherson's cabin near Athol?"

"I hadn't thought about that. It certainly could be. It could also be the address of Coxes' cabin."

"I didn't know they had a cabin," Monica said, somewhat surprised at my comment.

"I don't know, but it seems to be something we should find out."

"Maybe we should go to Massachusetts and check out the MacPherson cabin. Does anyone know you have the address?"

"No, I don't think so. Koato came into the carriage house after I found it and put it in my pocket.

"Tomorrow we'll go up to Knollwood's and have a talk with Bradford. We won't say anything about going to Athol. I still want to talk to a couple of the PIs on our list before we go to Athol. I'd like to know if any of them even know about the cabin."

"Sounds like a good idea," Monica agreed.

"Let's go back to the house. I hate to have poor Koato racking his brain trying to figure out what we've been talking about," I said with a smile.

"Okay, but I've had enough of reports for one night."

"Me, too."

We turned around and started back toward the house. I slipped my arm around Monica's waist as we slowly walked along the drive. I could see just a hint of someone in one of the upstairs windows. I glanced over at Monica and smiled.

"He's at it again," I said.

"Yeah. I can see him. I'll bet he reports everything we do."

"I'm sure he does."

As we got closer to the house, I began to wonder about how far Neil would go to keep an eye on us. It was time to be very cautious, and that included keeping an eye out for someone tailing us whenever we left the estate.

We entered the house to find Koato standing at the front door again. It seemed we couldn't go anywhere that he didn't show up.

"Koato, we will need the car first thing in the morning."

"Yes, sir. May I ask where you are going in case Mr. Cox would like to know?"

"Certainly. We are going to Knollwood's Resort and Casino to have a talk with his friend Bradford. It seems William had been there just a short time before he disappeared. We are just following up some of the information we found in the reports in the hope of finding something that might have been left out. I'm sure you understand," I said as I smiled at him.

"Yes, sir. I understand."

"We plan to leave early, so I think we will turn in."

"Would you like to have breakfast before you leave?"

"No. We'll get something along the way."

"Very well, sir," Koato said.

Monica and I went up the stairs to the second floor. As we turned to go down the hall, I glanced down toward the bottom of the stairs. Koato was standing there looking up at us. The look on his face gave me the impression that he might not have believed me, but I didn't care if he did or not.

As we entered the room, Monica knew enough not to say anything. We had no idea if the room was bugged or not, but we were not going to take the chance.

Monica went into the bathroom. When she came out she was wearing satin pajamas. I was a little surprised, but when

I thought about the room possibly being bugged, it was not too far a stretch to think it might have hidden cameras, too.

Monica looked at me. She knew I was used to her sleeping in the nude with me, but a nod of my head let her know I understood. I usually sleep in the nude, too, but tonight I wore my undershorts.

While getting ready for bed, we had kept our conversation limited to small unimportant things. I did mention that William had been tossed out of Knollwood's and I wanted to know more about the incident. If it was overheard, it would just reinforce our reason for going to Knollwood's. Besides, it didn't make any difference if they overheard us as it was part of the records Neil had already given us.

Once we were in bed, Monica shut off the bedside lamp and curled up beside me. We were both tired and didn't feel like making love with the possibility of someone hearing and watching us. I kissed her goodnight, then laid back and closed my eyes. It took awhile before I finally went to sleep.

CHAPTER ELEVEN

I woke rather early, even before the sun had come up. It must have been the thought that someone might be watching us. I glanced over at Monica and found her looking at me.

"You ready to get up?" I asked.

"Yes," she said then rolled over to me.

"Do you think there are cameras in the bathroom?" she whispered in my ear.

"I don't know, but if there are I will rip them out, toss them in the middle of the dining room table. I will tell them where they can go and, then we will leave. But right now, I think I will check it out."

I got out of bed and went into the bathroom. A complete search of the bathroom produced nothing that should concern either of us. As soon as I was done, I returned to the bedroom.

"Nothing," I said, then watched Monica go into the bathroom.

As soon as she was in the bathroom and had the door closed, I began a complete search of the bedroom for any type of surveillance equipment, audio or video. Monica came out of the bathroom and stood by the door. She watched me as I continued my search. She didn't say anything while she waited for me to finish.

"Nothing," I said. "The place is clean."

"My stomach was a little upset this morning," Monica said. "I think it really bothered me that someone might be spying on us."

"Are you all right now?" I asked.

"Yes, I think so."

"This makes me wonder if we are being spied on while we are working in the den. I have to wonder if it wasn't just our imagination."

"I don't know if it was our imagination or not, but I still don't feel comfortable in the house. There's just too much that doesn't seem to add up," Monica said. "I would rather be safe than sorry."

"I agree. We will still not say much in the house. Besides, a little walk while we talk about what we find is not a bad idea anyway. It might even help us make sense of what we find."

Monica nodded her head that she agreed, then began to gather what we would need for as much as a five day road trip. I had no idea how long we would be gone, but I wanted to be out of the house before Neil came home. He had said that he was staying overnight in the city because of a late meeting, but I had no idea if he was going to return in the morning or later in the day.

Once we were packed for our road trip, we left the room. When we got to the stairs, I noticed Koato standing at the bottom of the stairs waiting for us. I glanced at Monica before we started down the stairs.

"Your car is out front, sir," Koato said as he reached for our luggage.

"Thank you, but I can manage," I said while refusing to give him our luggage.

"Yes sir," he said then held the door for us.

I took our luggage and put them in the trunk of the car while Monica got in. I then walked around and got in the car behind the steering wheel. I started the car and headed down the drive. Koato was standing near the front door of the house watching us leave.

As I approached the front gate, it began to open. By the time I got to it, it was wide-open. I drove out onto the street and headed for the nearest entrance to the interstate highway that would take us toward Connecticut. We hadn't driven very far when a thought passed through my mind.

"Monica do you hear something strange?" I asked as a glanced at her.

Monica looked at me for a moment, then said, "Yes. I don't remember hearing it before."

"I think we better have it checked out. Keep an eye out for a service garage where we can get it checked out."

"There's one in the next block," Monica said, looking down the street.

"I see it."

I pulled into the service garage and got out of the car. A young man in coveralls came out of the building to greet us.

"Good morning," he said. "Can I help you?"

"Good morning. I was wondering if you have time to put this car on one of your hoists. I have a strange sound coming from under it. I would like you to see if you can find out what is making the noise."

"Sure."

I handed the young man the keys then walked around to the other side of the car. Once Monica was out of the car, the young man took the car and drove it into a bay and put it up on the hoist. I walked over to the man as I watched the car being raised up.

"I would like to take a look with you, if you don't mind?" I asked.

"I don't mind, but our insurance company does," he said.

"I understand, but we are not looking for something that makes a lot of noise. We are looking for a tracking bug," I said as I reached into my coat pocket and pulled out my Private Investigator's License.

He took a look at it, then nodded that he had no objections. We walked under the car and began looking for something that didn't belong there. It didn't take but a moment to find a tracking bug under the rear bumper. I pointed it out to the young man, then motioned for him to come with me. We walked over in the corner so I could talk to him without anyone being able to hear us.

"I don't want you to touch it. I want you to get the car down and park it over there with the other cars. I'm going to call the car rental agency and ask them to bring us a different car. When they do, they will take this one back with them. If anyone should ask, we brought the car in because of a strange noise in the transmission, but you didn't find anything. Okay?" I asked as I held out a twenty dollar bill.

"Yeah, sure," he said as he took the twenty.

"I want you to make out a bill for your inspection of the car. I'll pay you for it."

"Okay," he replied then went to his office and made out the bill.

I paid the bill and then called the car rental agency. After a brief explanation of why we wanted a different car, they agreed to bring us one. While I was on the phone, the young man took the car off the hoist and parked it with the other cars that were waiting to be serviced or had already been serviced.

While we waited for a new car, we went across the street to a little café for breakfast. We sat at a table by a front window so I could keep an eye on the street. I was watching for someone who drove by the service garage more than once, or someone who parked near the service garage and didn't leave their car. I saw an SUV that had gone by the service garage twice before it was parked just down the street. No one got out of the SUV.

When we finished eating, we returned to the service garage to wait for the car. We sat down in the waiting room where I could continue to watch the SUV.

"Well, I think we have found our tail. It's the dark green SUV parked in the next block at the corner" I said. "It has two men in it. I'm not a hundred percent sure, but I think one of them looks like Neil's bodyguard."

"Won't they see us when we leave and follow us?" Monica asked.

"Sure, but now we know the vehicle is following us. It will not be hard to ditch them whenever we're ready."

"Do you think they will follow us or the car when it is taken away?"

"It would be nice if they follow the car we drove in here, but if they see that it was driven away by someone other than us they are not likely to follow it. They are more likely to be watching us now so they follow the right car."

Monica didn't say anything more. She sat in the waiting room and flipped thought a couple of magazines while I kept an eye on the SUV. I knew she wasn't reading anything in them. She was just trying to relax which was not easy for her.

When the new car arrived, I signed the papers for it, then transferred our luggage to it. We got in and I started the car as soon as Monica had settled in and fastened her seatbelt.

"Hang on," I said with a smile.

Monica looked at me as if she expected me to take off like we were on fire. I turned out on the street in the opposite direction that our tail was pointed. It meant he would have to make a U-turn in the middle of a busy street. Not an easy thing to do if he wanted to stay with us.

I glanced back in the rearview mirror as I approached a corner. They were just making the U-turn. I turned the corner and darted down the street to the middle of the block then turned into an alley. They had not seen us turn into the alley. Part way down the alley was the back of a parking lot. I turned and drove through the parking lot and out onto the next street and headed in the direction we had been going. At the next corner, I turned and headed for the next corner where I turned again. I was pretty sure that we had lost them. I continued on down the street keeping an eye out for them behind me. After traveling several blocks without seeing the SUV, I figured I had lost them.

"I think that will keep them off our backs for a little while," I said.

"Won't they just go back to Cox's and ask Koato where we were going?"

"They might if it was Koato who put them on us in the first place, but it won't do them any good," I said as I glanced over at Monica.

"Why not?"

"We're not going to Knollwood's first. We are going to pay visits to a couple of private investigators, and we are going to take a little trip up to Massachusetts."

"Are we going to MacPherson's cabin near Athol?"

"Yes," I said just as I came up with another thought. "I wonder. Do the Coxes have a cabin somewhere? It's never been mentioned."

"I don't know," Monica said.

"I think we should find out. If they do, it might not be a bad idea if we find out where Coxes' cabin is and check it out."

"How do you plan to do that?" Monica asked.

"I think we will ask some of the PIs who have worked on the case. One of them might know. We can also ask Bradford when we get there. Since he is a good friend of Neil's, he might know."

"That sounds like a good idea."

Monica didn't say anything for sometime. She just sat and watched the miles go by. It was almost noon when we crossed the state line from Connecticut into Massachusetts.

"How are we going to find MacPherson's cabin? We have no idea where it is located."

"I'm going to stop in at the local police station and talk to whoever might be there," I replied.

* * * *

The drive to Athol was a very nice drive. There were a lot of wooded areas, and we passed a number of lakes and streams. It seemed like the sort of place one would visit to get away from the hustle and bustle of the big city. Even Athol looked like a lazy little town.

"This isn't much of a town. The sign says only five hundred and thirty people live here," Monica said as we drove by the village limit sign announcing the fact that we were in Athol.

"I'm hoping that will make it easier to find their cabin. Over there, the gas station," I said. "It looks like a good place to start."

I pulled into the gas station and stopped next to one of the pumps. An elderly gentleman came out and walked over to us.

"Howdy folks. What can I do for you?"

"I see the pumps don't have a place for credit cards."

"Nope. I still pump the gas. Have been for forty years," he said with a smile.

"Okay. You can fill it up."

"Sure enough."

I watched the old man as he began to fill the gas tank. He seemed very comfortable with himself. He washed the windshield and even wiped off the headlights.

"What brings you folks up this way?" he asked without looking at me.

"We are looking for the MacPherson cabin. You wouldn't happen to know where it is would you?"

"Sure enough, but there ain't no one there this week."

"Oh. We were to meet James at the cabin."

"Well, now he might be there. He's not like his folks. He doesn't always stop in before he goes to the cabin," the old man said. "His folks always stop by to get a few things before they head out to their cabin. Mr. and Mrs.

MacPherson were always real nice people. They're not so uppity as James."

"I would have to agree with you on that," I said with a smile. "Then it is possible James might be at the cabin?"

"Yeah. He might. Mr. MacPherson died about three years ago. Ain't seen Mrs. MacPherson since."

"How do I find the cabin?"

"Well, you just go back about a mile and half down the same road you come into town on. You'll see a dirt road that goes off to the right toward the lake. Go down that road until you come to another dirt road. That's the road to their cabin. You can't miss the place. It's right at the end of the road."

"Thank you for your help. How much do I owe you?"

"That'll be thirty-five dollars and fifty-five cents."

I handed the old man forty dollars and told him to keep the change. He thanked us, and we got back in the car and headed back the way we came.

At about a mile and a half we found a dirt road off to our right. We turned on the road and continued on. It seemed like forever before we came to another dirt road with a small sign that read "MacPhersons". We turned on the narrow dirt road.

It was a good six or seven miles before we saw anything other than trees and an occasional marshy area. I slowed down at the sight of a building in among the trees. I pulled off the road and stopped. I could see a car parked alongside the building.

"What do you think?" Monica asked.

"I think someone is here."

"Do you think James might be here?"

"I don't know what kind of a car James drives, but the car has not been here very long. You can see where it pushed the grass down. It hasn't straightened up again."

"What do we do now?"

I took a minute to look around. It was a pretty heavily forested area. The building I could see was obviously not the cabin. It looked more like a long narrow barn like the kind that horses would be kept in, but I didn't see anything to indicate there were any horses around. In fact, I was sure that there had not been any horses here for sometime as the paddocks next to the barn were covered with fairly tall grass and weeds.

"I think we'll leave the car and go on foot from here," I said. "Let's see if we can find the cabin."

I got out of the car and closed the door quietly. Monica followed my lead. She closed her door quietly, too. She met me at the front of the car. I pointed toward the back of the barn.

We started working our way around behind the barn. When we got to other end of the barn, I peeked around the corner. I could see the back of a rather large log home. From the looks of it, it was not a new home. It had probably been built in the late twenties or early thirties as a hunting and fishing lodge for someone of wealth. The front of the cabin faced toward a rather large lake. The area in front of the cabin was well mowed and had had a lot of care to make it look nice.

"Mia said James had a car that was not as nice as William's car. The car by the barn was newer then William's car. The car is pretty nice, but probably not considered as nice as William's classic Jag," I said. "I think James is here."

"What do we do now?"

"I think it might be a good time to confront him. I seriously doubt that he has any of his lawyers way out here."

"Okay. I'm ready," Monica said.

I smiled at her, then started walking toward the front of the house. Monica and I had just gotten to the front porch, and I was reaching up to knock on the screen door when I heard the backdoor slam shut. I glanced at Monica for just a second, then took off at a run around toward the back of the house.

As I came around the corner, I saw James running toward his car. He had a young woman in tow. I continued to chase them toward the car, but he had too much of a lead on me. By the time I got to the barn, they were in the car and James was making good time at getting out of there. I did manage to get a look at the girl's face when she looked out the car window to see if I might catch them. It was only a matter of seconds before they disappeared down the road.

There was no sense in trying to catch them. I was too far from our car, so I turned around and walked back to join Monica. She was waiting for me at the back of the cabin.

"Did you get a good look at the young woman?" Monica asked.

"Yes," I said as I tried to catch my breath.

"Any idea who the young woman was?"

"I think it was Susan Small. I'm not real sure. The only time I've seen a picture of her was on the tapes at Knollwood's."

"That was the waitress at Knollwood's who served William?"

"Yes. And according to Sam, she was William's girlfriend."

"I thought she was in California."

"That's what we were told. But it appears she either came back or someone lied to us and the other investigators. I'd be willing to bet that someone lied. I have a feeling that she never went to California," I said as I turned and looked at the cabin.

"What's next?"

"I'm going to take a look around the cabin. I got a feeling that Ms. Small has been living here for sometime. The only question is, was she here alone or with someone."

I turned and headed for the backdoor of the cabin. Monica was right behind me. Once inside, I went from room to room looking for any clues that would help me find William or what might have happened to him. I was also looking for something that would give me an idea of how long Ms. Small had been living there.

After spending a good deal of time searching the house, the only thing I found was nothing. The girl had obviously lived there for sometime, but it was hard to tell just how long. She could have been there for a couple of weeks or for much longer. There was little chance anyone would have known she was there.

"What do you think?" Monica asked.

"This place is so far out of the way, there is little likelihood that anyone would know she was here. There are a few clothes hung up in the closet, but there are some clothes still in suitcases. There's just no way to tell how long she might have been here," I said with a hint of frustration.

"What about food in the kitchen? Wouldn't it give you a clue as to how long she might have been here?"

"I looked in the cupboards, but I didn't see anything that would help determine how long she had been here," I said. "The interesting thing to me is what was she doing here with James?"

"I guess we need to ask James that," Monica said.

I looked around the room, then walked over to the front door. After making sure it was locked, I took Monica by the arm and we left out the backdoor. I made sure the backdoor was locked before we walked back to the car.

After we were in the car, I looked at Monica and said, "I think we're done here for now. Our next stop is back in Connecticut. I want to talk to the investigator from Hartford. What was his name?"

Monica took a minute to check our notes before she came up with his name.

"His name is Buck Matthews."

"I think we should start there, then work our way back to Knollwood's."

"Okay," Monica said.

I started the car, turned it around then headed back toward the highway. Once we were back on the highway, Monica leaned back in the seat and rested her eyes while I drove.

CHAPTER TWELVE

After a short stop for lunch we continued on toward Connecticut. It was late afternoon when we finally arrived in Hartford. We stopped at a tourist center where we could get a map of the city. It didn't take us very long to find out where Buck Matthews Investigation Agency was located. It was located at the end of a small strip mall. I pulled in and parked in front of Buck Matthews's office.

The office of Buck Matthews Investigation Agency didn't look like much, but then our office was in our home. We got out of the car and walked up to the door. I held the door for Monica then followed her in. We were greeted by a nice looking young woman sitting at a desk. It looked like she was playing games on the computer.

"Can I help you with something?" she asked as she chewed her gum.

"Yes. We would like to talk to Mr. Buck Matthews, please."

"Have a seat," she said.

We sat down and watched the young woman as she got up and walked through a door into an office. It was just a moment before a man walked out of the office toward us. He looked to be in his mid-fifties and in pretty good shape. He was wearing a gray suit with a red tie. If we had been in a different office, I might have mistaken him for a banker.

"I'm Buck Matthews," he said as he reached out a hand to me.

"Nick McCord. This is my wife and partner, Monica," I said as I shook his hand.

"Very nice to meet you," he said as he looked at Monica and smiled. "Please, come in."

He motioned us to his office, then followed us in. He motioned toward the chairs in front of his desk, then waited for us to sit down.

"What is it I can do for you folks?"

"We are investigators from Wisconsin. It is our understanding that you did some work for Mr. Neil Cox. You had been hired to find his son, I believe."

"That's right. What's your interest in the case? Has Mr. Cox hired you to find his kid?"

"Yes."

"Well, good luck," he said with a hint of sarcasm.

"We have been looking over some of your reports that you gave Neil. We would like to ask you a few questions about them."

"Sure. Fire away."

"We got the impression that you were making some progress in the case. Can you tell us why Neil fired you?"

"I have no idea. Like you said, I was making some progress in the case. I had stopped by to tell him that I thought I had a pretty good lead. I was really encouraged with it."

"If you had a good lead, why didn't he let you follow it up?" I asked.

"I don't know. He never told me why he fired me, but I later found out he had fired a couple of other investigators before me. That sort of thing gets around, you know. It got so that none of the investigators in this area would even talk to him, but I see he went out of state to find someone to make him look like he was trying to find his son."

"Do you really think that he is just making it look like he's trying to find William?" I asked.

"Yes, I do. And so do a couple of other investigators I know."

"In looking over the reports from some of the other investigators and having talked to one of them, I have to agree with you. Is there anything you can tell me about your investigation that might help us? Maybe just a feeling or a hunch you had about the case."

"With what you know, are you going to continue to look for his son?"

Buck seemed surprised that we would continue. I got the impression he thought we might be a little nuts.

"Yes. There is too much going on here that needs to be investigated. I've got a strong feeling Neil is hiding something. It's almost as if he knows where his son is, but doesn't want his wife or anyone else to know."

"I agree with you, but what can you do if he fires you?"

"Monica and I have discussed that very thing. We decided that we are going to take this investigation as far as we can in an effort to find William, with or without Neil's cooperation." I said.

"It could end up costing you a pretty penny."

"It could, but I think there is something going on that is probably illegal, or most assuredly is not right."

"Well, I'm not busy at the moment, so, what can I do to help, Nick?"

"Answer a few questions, for a starter."

"Sure," he said with a little more enthusiasm.

"Did you ever interview Susan Small?"

"No. I did interview her mother and step-father. I got nothing out of them. They told me that she had gone to California, but in following it up I found nothing to indicate that she went anywhere."

"What was your feeling about it?"

"I don't think she even left the state. If she did, it wasn't very far," he said. "Certainly not to California."

"I don't know if she went to California or not, but I saw her yesterday at MacPherson's cabin in Massachusetts."

"No kidding? The MacPherson cabin near Athol?"

"Right. She was with James MacPherson."

"That's interesting."

"We thought so," I said.

"I interviewed him, if you could call it that," Buck said. "He had two high-powered lawyers from New York City doing most of the talking for him. You can just about guess what I got out of him."

"Nothing," I said with a grin.

"You got that right."

"I got a little out of him with the threat of having him hauled out of his office in cuffs in front of his fellow employees. But the more I find out, the more I know it was a lie."

"When I interviewed MacPherson he seemed very nervous," Buck said.

"Same here. Can you tell me if Cox has a cabin somewhere?"

"Yeah. He has one in northwestern Massachusetts. I'm not sure where, but from what I was able to gather it's somewhere near Windsor. There's some pretty country up that way. I think it was an old hunting or fishing lodge at one time or at least it's the place where he used to go hunting. I'm not sure if he even uses it anymore."

"How did you find out about it?"

"I stumbled onto it when I was talking with some old guy that knew about it. He couldn't tell me where it was, but he knew it was near Windsor, Massachusetts. I'd put you on to the old guy, but he died almost a year ago."

"I should be able to find out where it is if Neil hasn't sold it."

"Good luck with that," Buck said.

"Did you try to find his cabin?"

"No. He fired me before I had a chance to figure out where it was," Buck said. "I guess you could say I was mad enough to drop the whole thing, because that is just what I did. I collected my pay and went home. By the way, he paid me a good size bonus when he fired me. I think it was his way to insure I didn't continue my search for William."

"He paid off the others to end their searches, too," I said.

"I know. I've talked to a couple of them."

"Did you ever talk to Marcus Longmont?" I asked.

"Yeah. He's a New York City cop."

"What did you think of him?"

"I'm not sure," Buck said thoughtfully. "He seems okay, but he wasn't near as much help as I would have expected from a detective who works in Missing Persons. His answers to my questions were rather vague. It was almost as if he didn't want to talk to me. It might have been the fact I'm a PI. There's a lot of cops out there that don't like us," he said with a grin.

"Yeah. I know what you mean," I said. "Is there anything else you can think of that might help us?"

"Not at the moment," he said after a moment of thought. "What's your next move?"

"I'm not sure. "I'm going over to Knollwood's and talk to Sam Bradford again to see if he found anything on his spy cameras," I said with a chuckle.

"Bradford's a good man."

"Yes, he is. I've worked with him before."

"Say "Hi" to him for me."

"Will do," I said as I stood up. "If you think of anything else, I would appreciate it if you would give me a call."

I gave him one of my cards as I shook his hand. Monica stood up beside me and offered her hand to him.

"It was nice meeting you, Mrs. McCord. I don't often get such beautiful women in my office."

"Well, thank you," Monica said with a smile that would melt butter.

We turned and left Buck's office. Once we were in the car, I sat behind the wheel and looked out the windshield at the front of Buck's office.

"What's on your mind, Nick?"

"What is your opinion of Mr. Matthews?"

"I don't know. He seems like an all right sort of guy. I got the feeling he was pretty straight forward with us. He seems to know what he's doing. Why? Is something bothering you?"

"No, not really. Maybe it's just the way he seemed to do things."

"What do you mean?"

"I wonder why he told Neil that he had a good lead before he followed it up. That seemed to be the reason Neil fired him. I would have followed up the lead and then told Neil about it if it proved important," I said.

"I see what you mean. Maybe he believed Neil should be aware of what he was doing. After all, he was paying the investigators pretty well."

"I guess you're right. I just do things a little differently."

I looked at Monica and then started the car. I backed out of the parking space and stopped.

"Where to now?" Monica asked.

"Do we have another PI in this area to talk to?"

"Let me check," Monica said as she opened her note pad.

I glanced over at Monica and saw her going through the list. It wasn't long and she had figured it out.

"Okay, we have talked to two of the six investigators Neil hired in Connecticut. We thought that only four might have something to tell us. One in Stamford and one in Hartford. There are two who seemed to just send Neil a bill but didn't do anything. The other two we wanted to talk to are in New Haven and New London. New London is not very far from Knollwood's, and New Haven would be on our way back to Long Island," Monica said.

"There is another one in the Hartford area that was questionable. He appeared to take the case seriously for a while, then he just stopped sending Neil reports," Monica added.

"Where is he located?"

"He is located in Glastonbury. That's south of here. We would have to backtrack a ways if you think we should try to find Cox's cabin first. We could see him on the way back. Glastonbury is on Highway 2. That would be on our way to Knollwood's."

"Let's stop in and see him on the way back if we decide he's worth the stop. Right now, I think we should head toward Windsor, Massachusetts," I said.

"I think we should find a coffee shop where we can figure out a route to Windsor," Monica suggested.

We left the strip mall parking lot and drove down the street. It didn't take me very long to find a nice little coffee shop. We took our maps and went inside. We found a table out of the way and sat down. A teenage girl came over and asked us what we would like. After giving her our order, we spread the map out on the table.

"I think we should plot a course from Knollwood's to Windsor, Massachusetts. On second thought, make it from New London to Windsor," I said. "I want to intersect it on our way north, then follow it to Windsor."

"What's on your mind?"

"Didn't Susan Small live in New London?"

"No. She lived in Avery Hill."

"Okay. Make it from Avery Hill to Windsor."

"I take it you want to go to Windsor to see if we can find Cox's cabin?"

"I do. I would like to see the place."

"Do you think William is there?"

"I don't know. It's just a hunch. If William is there, we might find James and Susan there as well."

"So we are playing a hunch?"

"That's about it. Do you have a better idea?"

"No. Since we can see the other PIs anytime; and we are closer to Windsor now, why not?" she said with a grin.

"I want you to find me a route that would run along the same highways William might have taken if he picked up Susan and headed for the lodge at Windsor in the most direct way."

"Okay," Monica said as she started to figure out the route to Windsor.

When our coffee came, I sat next to Monica and watched her as she laid out a route. The first thing I noticed was that we would be going back the way we came for the first leg of the trip to Windsor.

"It will be a long trip to Windsor for so late in the day. I think we should probably spend the night somewhere along the way," Monica said.

"Any suggestions on where you would like to stop?"

"I think it might be a good idea to see if we can find a place just north of Springfield, maybe at Northampton just off Interstate 91. It looks like it might be the last major town before we get to the highway that goes northwest to Windsor."

"Okay. I think we should get going."

We finished our coffee, and left the coffee shop. I drove out onto Interstate 91 and headed north. Monica tipped back in the seat and closed her eyes. She looked rather comfortable.

As the miles went by, I wondered what we might find once we got to Windsor. From what I had seen on the map, it didn't look like there was much in the way of population in that part of Massachusetts. Since I didn't know much about the area, I had no idea what we might find. The map hinted that it was probably fairly hilly with areas of thick forests.

My thought was reinforced by the fact that the map showed several Scenic routes in the area.

* * * *

It was well past dinner time when we pulled into a Hampton Inn in the Northampton area. Monica waited in the car while I went inside to see if there was a place for us at the Inn. They had a very nice room for us. I registered us then returned to the car. After parking the car, we gathered our overnight bags and went to our room.

Once we were ready, we left the Inn and went down the street to a restaurant for dinner. We had an excellent meal, then returned to the Inn. It was getting late and neither of us wanted to watch any television.

"I could use a shower," I said.

"Me, too," Monica said with a sexy smile. "Do you mind if I take one with you?"

"Not at all."

It didn't take us very long to get out of our clothes. I took her by the hand and led her into the bathroom. She waited while I turned on the shower and made sure it was not too hot or too cold. I then reached out for her hand and stepped into the shower. She stepped in, and moved up to me. She put her arms around my neck while I slipped my hands around her narrow waist. I pulled her up against me. It felt good holding her against me. Her body was warm and firm, yet her skin was so soft. She felt good under my hands.

Monica moaned softly as I slid my hand up and down her smooth back. It had seemed like forever since I had held her so close. I got the feeling from the way she held me that she felt the same way. She finally let go of me and reached for the soap. We washed each other, then rinsed off.

It wasn't long before we were ready to get out of the shower. As soon as we dried off, I went to the bed. I pulled the covers down, then picked her up and laid her on the bed. I laid down beside her and curled up with her. We took sometime to just cuddle and kiss each other. It wasn't long before we were feeling our desire for each other grow into passion.

"Nick, I want you to make love to me," she said in a whisper.

I kissed her again then wrapped her in my arms. I don't know how long we spent making love to each other. All I know was that we fell asleep in each others' arms and had one of the most peaceful sleeps we had had in sometime.

CHAPTER THIRTEEN

I woke as the sun started to creep in around the ends of the drapes in our room. Monica was lying against my back. I could feel her soft warm breath on the back of my neck, and her arm resting over me. I didn't want to move if she was still sleeping. It wasn't long and I felt Monica's hand move softly over my chest.

"You ready to get up?" I asked.

"No, but I think we should," she replied.

There was something about the way she responded to my question that made me think there might be a problem.

"Are you all right?" I asked as I rolled over so I could look at her.

"I'm not sure. My stomach is a little upset this morning. I think I'm just a bit hungry."

"What can I do for you?"

"Nothing. I should be all right once I get something in my stomach."

"Okay. Let's get dressed and go have breakfast."

Monica nodded that she agreed with me. I rolled out of bed and went into the bathroom. When I came out, Monica was sitting on the edge of the bed. She smiled up at me, then stood up. I walked up to her and took her in my arms. She wrapped her arms around my neck and smiled up at me.

"I think I know what's making me feel sick in the morning."

"What? I hope it's not me," I said as I smiled at her and slid my hand down over her bare behind.

"In a way, it is you," she said with a grin. "I think I might be pregnant."

"Are you sure?" I said with a bit of a surprise.

"No, but I think I should see a doctor when we get home."

"Should we go home now?"

"No. We can continue with our investigation. It will be awhile before we have to worry about what I do."

"Are you sure?"

"Yes, I'm sure," she said with a big grin. "I'll just watch what I eat until I see my doctor back home."

"Okay, but if you think you need to go home, just say the word and I'll take you home."

"I'll be fine. If you'll let go of me, I'll get dressed so we can go get breakfast."

I leaned down and kissed her, then let go of her. I watched her as she walked into the bathroom. When she came out I was dressed and ready to go. I found it hard not to watch her as she got dressed. She didn't seem to be excited about the prospect of being a mother, but she had a glow about her. It was probably my imagination, but it seemed real enough.

As soon as she was ready, we left the room. We had breakfast in the lounge, paid our motel bill, then retrieved our luggage. After putting it in the car, we headed out for Route 9 toward Windsor. I found it hard not to look over at her to make sure that she was doing okay.

"Nick, how do you feel about having a baby?"

At that moment, I wasn't really sure how to answer her question. The thought of having a child made all sorts of questions run through my mind. For one thing, I knew it would change everything.

"It's really hard to say. There are a lot of things to think about. There will be a lot of changes in our lives with a baby. As far as being a father, I think I would be a good father. I know I will certainly love our baby."

Monica smiled as she looked at me. I could tell she was happy to know that I would love our child.

"Do you want a boy or a girl?" Monica asked.

"It really doesn't matter. All I would hope for is a healthy child, but no matter what, we will love our baby."

"I would like to have your baby," Monica said as she reached over and rested her hand on my leg.

"I would like you to have my baby, too," I said as I glanced at her. "But right now, I think I had better pay attention. The road to Windsor should be coming up very soon."

"There it is. Highway 9," Monica said.

I got off the interstate and turned onto Highway 9. It was a pretty good two lane highway.

"It turns into a scenic route at Lithia until East Windsor. We continue on Highway 9 to Windsor," Monica said as she looked at the map. "It's about five more miles to Windsor."

The trip from Northampton to Windsor was a very pleasant drive. There were lots of forests and scenic areas along the way. It didn't take us very long to get to Windsor. As we drove into town, we found it was very small. There were only a few shops which included a small grocery store, a cafe and a gas station. I pulled into the gas station and got out of the car. A man in his mid-fifties came out.

"Hi, folks. What can I do for you?"

"We are looking for the cabin of Neil Cox. Would you happen to know where it is located?"

"The Cox lodge is about two and a half miles north of here on Route 8A. Just after you cross the bridge over the river, there's a turn off to the right. It's back in there about a mile or so."

"Thank you," I said.

"Might I ask what your interest in Mr. Cox's lodge is?"

"I was thinking about looking it over and maybe making an offer on the property. I heard it was deserted."

"Yeah, it is deserted. Mr. and Mrs. Cox haven't been up here since the lodge burned down a little over – ah – about five years ago or there abouts," he said thoughtfully.

I had no idea the lodge had burned down, but I wasn't about to let him know that.

"Are there any other buildings still standing on the property?"

"Yeah. There's a barn and a small cabin that they sometimes used for a handyman who would work there in the summer. Nobody's been up there since the lodge burned down except for insurance people a couple of times. There's no tellin' what condition the cabin and barn are in."

"Have you been out there?"

"I haven't been out there since the last time there was an insurance man out there to appraise the damage. I took him out to the place. There were a lot of old antiques that burned up in the fire. There were a number of us here in town who thought Mr. Cox was going to rebuild it, but nothin's been done."

"What kind of antiques were in the lodge?"

"I'm not rightly sure, but from what the insurance man said there must have been a lot. I think Mr. Cox was storing them at the lodge."

"When was the last time an insurance appraiser was out there?"

"I can't say for sure, but the last time I knew about one being there was about a month or so after it burned, maybe a bit longer."

"Did you talk to the appraiser?"

"Yeah, sure."

"Did he have anything to say about the antiques?"

"Not really, but he did mention that the antiques were worth more than the lodge."

"Thanks."

"Are you still going out there?"

"Yes. I think I'll look around a bit. Never know, it might be just what I'm looking for," I said with a smile.

He nodded as if he understood, then turned and went back into the station. I got back in the car and sat there looking out the windshield. I wondered why we had not been told about the lodge or the fact that it had burned down, and about the antiques that burned in it. The fact it had burned down a little over five years ago seemed to me to be a rather important piece of information. I wondered if it had burned down before or after William disappeared. Another thought was did the fire have anything to do with William's disappearance.

"What did you find out?" Monica asked.

"Neil not only failed to tell us about his country lodge, he failed to tell us it burned down over five years ago. He also didn't tell us that there were a lot of antiques destroyed in the fire."

"It burned down? Maybe he thought that since it had burned down there was no need to mention it. Without the lodge, William would not be able to use the lodge for a place to hide out," Monica said.

"Apparently not so. According to the gentleman I just talked to, there are a cabin and a barn still standing on the property."

"So there's still a place for him to hold up there."

"Right. I think we need to pay the Cox lodge a visit," I said.

I reached down and started the car. I found where route 8A headed north out of town. It wasn't long before we came to a bridge over a river. I slowed the car as I crossed over the bridge and looked for a turn off to the right. The turn off was just a narrow dirt road that looked more like a two lane cow path. It also looked like it had not been used for sometime. There were weeds and grass growing up in the middle of the road. I stopped the car and looked down the road.

"I'm going to take a look around," I said as I opened the door.

"What are you looking for?" Monica asked.

"Tracks, tire tracks."

I walked around in front of the car and studied the bare spots in the road. I didn't really expect to find anything, but it certainly wouldn't hurt to look. If I found any tracks it might give me an idea of how long it had been since the road had been used.

At first I didn't see any tracks at all, but I noticed there were some sort of marks across the bare spots in the road. Kneeling down for a closer look, I got the impression that someone had tried to brush away the tracks with a branch. I wondered what they were trying to hide. It had obviously been done by someone who didn't know what they were doing.

I turned and motioned for Monica to follow me with the car. I then turned and continued to walk along the road. I hadn't gone more that about a hundred feet or so when I spotted tracks. I knelt down to study them. It looked like tracks from a car, but with my limited knowledge of tire tracks I wasn't sure. It could have been from a pickup truck. All I was sure of was that someone had driven down the road fairly recently. The fact that some of the tracks had been wiped out, convinced me that whoever tried to wipe out the tracks didn't want anyone to know they had been out to the Coxes' lodge. I returned to the car.

"Someone has been down this road recently, and they didn't want anyone to know about it."

"You think it might have been William?" Monica asked.

"I don't know, but there is only one set of tracks. That would indicate whoever drove down the road is still down there," I said. "That is unless there is another way out of here."

"What are we going to do?"

"We are going to drive on down the road to Cox's lodge."

Monica went around to the other side of the car and got in. I got in behind the wheel, put the car in gear and drove on down the road rather slowly. I had no idea what might be ahead of us, but I wanted no surprises.

The road followed along the edge of a tree line. There was a fairly heavy forest on one side of the road and a long, rather narrow meadow on the other. We must have gone about a half a mile before the road turned into the forest. I stopped to look around before driving into the forest. The road looked like it wound around in the forest. I could not see any buildings from the edge of the woods.

"What now?" Monica asked.

"I'm not sure. The tracks indicate that someone might be back in there. Since I have no idea who it might be, I want to be cautious. I think it would be a good idea if we walk from here. You feel like a walk in the woods with me?" I asked as I looked at Monica.

"Sure. I could use a little exercise," she said with a smile.

I pulled our car off the road. We got out of the car. I checked the road to make sure the tire tracks I had seen earlier continued on down the road. As soon as I was sure the vehicle had continued into the woods, we started walking along the edge of the road just inside the woods. We hadn't walked very far when I reached out and stopped Monica.

"There's a small building back in the woods. I'm not sure what it is, but we need to be careful," I whispered.

I took her hand and led her deeper into the woods where it would be harder for someone to see us. We started working our way toward the small building using the trees and underbrush for cover. It wasn't long and we had gotten close enough to see that the building was nothing more than a storage shed. Leaving Monica behind a large bush, I worked my way closer to the back of the shed and looked in a small window on the back wall.

There was a small tractor with a blade on the back. It looked like it might have been used to grade the road to the lodge. I couldn't see anything other than a number of tools. There was also a riding mower. I looked at Monica and motioned for her to come. She moved up beside me.

"It's nothing but a tool shed," I whispered to Monica.

"Does it look like anything has been used lately?"

"I can't tell. Let's continue on, but keep a look out for anyone or any other buildings."

Monica nodded that she understood. I turned and carefully moved around to the side of the shed where I took a minute to scan the area. I was looking for any sign of a building of any kind or for anyone who might be around. Since I didn't see anyone, I took Monica's hand and started working our way through the trees. We continued to stay deep enough in the woods that it would be hard to see us, but not so far back we couldn't see the road.

The road made a sudden turn. As we turned to follow along the edge of the road, I could see a small cabin back in the woods on the other side of the road. I pulled up short and looked at the cabin. I was trying to see if anyone was around. Monica moved up alongside me.

"See anyone?" Monica asked in a whisper.

"No, but I think someone is around, maybe inside."

"What makes you think that?" Monica asked.

"There's a paper cup on the porch railing."

Before we could decide what to do, James came running out of the cabin and took off down the road. Susan Small ran out of the cabin right behind him. With the distance between us, they had a pretty good head start.

I took off after James. I had no idea where he was going, but he was making pretty good time. Susan was unable to keep up with him. I could hear Monica running behind me.

Suddenly Susan tripped on a tree branch laying in the grass and fell. I ran right by her in my effort to catch James.

"Grab Susan," I yelled out to Monica as I continued after James.

James still had a good lead on me when he ran around behind what looked like a garage. As I approached the garage, I could hear the sound of a car start up. When I was only a few yards from the front of the garage, a car came crashing out right through the garage doors. I only had time to jump out of the way to avoid being run over.

I turned around in time to see James take off down the road. Since he didn't go down the road we had come up, it was clear that he must know the road came out somewhere else. There was nothing I could do, but watch him disappear from sight. All I could think of was that it was the second time James had gotten away from me.

I turned and looked toward where Susan had fallen. Monica was standing over Susan to make sure she didn't get away. I walked back to them.

"Please don't kill me," Susan begged as she looked up at me with tears rolling down her cheeks.

"I'm not here to kill you. I just want to talk to you," I said.

Susan looked from me to Monica, then back to me. She had a confused look on her face.

"Who told you we wanted to kill you?" I asked.

"James," she said in almost a whisper.

I looked at Monica. She glanced at me. What Susan had said didn't make any sense. James knew we were looking for William. Why would he tell Susan we were out to kill her?

"Nick, I think she sprained her ankle. Why don't you carry her into the cabin so I can take a look at it and get an ice pack on it?"

"Sure."

When I reached down to pick her up, she cowed back.

"I'm not going to hurt you," I said, then reached down to pick her up.

She still looked scared, but she didn't resist. I carried her into the cabin and sat her down on the bed. When I looked at her, she still looked very frightened. I backed away from the bed and sat down at the small table while Monica knelt down in front of Susan. She wrapped Susan's ankle with a tea towel and put some ice she found in the refrigerator on it.

"Susan, we are not here to kill anyone. We are here to find William. Mr. Cox hired us to find William, that's all," I said.

"Mr. Cox doesn't want William found, he wants him dead," she blurted out.

"What makes you say that?"

"He hates William."

"Why does he hate William?"

"Because William knows what he did."

I looked over at Monica. She was looking at me. This put a whole new spin on things.

"Do you know where William is?"

"No," she said quietly as she looked down at the floor.

"Okay. I will not ask you where William is again. I need you to tell me what it is William knows that makes his father hate him so much he wants his son dead."

"I can't tell you," she said, the look in her eyes showing the fear she felt.

"Why can't you tell us? We can protect you."

"No one can protect me. James told me that Mr. Cox has people looking for me," she said as she sniffled.

"Okay."

"Susan, you loved William, didn't you?" Monica asked, her voice soft and caring.

"I still do," she insisted.

"Do you know if William is still alive?"

Susan looked at Monica. Tears began to fill her eyes and roll down her cheeks. There was little doubt she knew, or at least suspected that William was dead. It had been five years since he had disappeared, but how long had it been since she had last seen him?

"Susan, when was the last time you saw William?" I asked.

"A little more than three years ago."

"You've been hiding out for five years?"

"William and I came up here about five years ago. We stayed in this cabin over a year. James would bring us supplies every once in awhile. William would hunt to provide us with meat. We have a storage shed back in the woods where we would hide everything. At first, we only used the cabin as a place to sleep and to cook. But after almost a year went by and no one came around, we sort of moved into the cabin, but we still had to keep an eye out for strangers."

"I take it William left at some point?" I asked.

"Yes. After we had been here for a little over a year, William went to talk to his father in the hope that we could return to a normal life, a life without all the hiding. I begged him not to go, but he said we would never have a life of our own if he didn't settle things with his father," Susan said then she began to cry.

"He never returned, did he?" Monica said softly.

"No," Susan replied, then broke down and cried openly.

Monica sat next to Susan on the bed and held her while she cried. I had no idea what I should do. I wasn't sure there was anything I could do. I couldn't tell her if William was alive or dead, because I didn't know. I couldn't take her back home because I didn't know if there was someone out there who was looking to kill her. I certainly couldn't let Neil know we had found her because I didn't know if he was out to kill her like she said. There were just too many unanswered questions. The one question that would help me the most was what was it that Neil had done to make his son run for his life.

I decided to go for a walk and look around. I had no idea what I was looking for, but I had a lot of small bits of information I needed to put together. The biggest piece of the puzzle was, what did William know about his father that made him run and hide.

As I stepped out on the porch of the cabin, I took a minute to look around. I wasn't really looking for anything in particular, just looking while I was thinking. Off in the woods across the road from the cabin, I could make out what looked like the remains of a burned-out building. I decided to walk over to it and look around while I was thinking.

When I came out of the woods, there was a large burned-out building. It had to be the lodge. The only thing left of it were a few charred logs sticking up a few feet above the ground and part of a very large porch. It was easy to see the outline of the building, but everything inside of it had been destroyed. I walked up close to the remains of the lodge and looked at the pile of rubble. It was clear that the lodge had not had a basement. I could see several places where weeds had taken hold and were starting to grow in among the charred remains.

It was at that moment I noticed what seemed to be something shiny about three or four feet into the rubble. I had no idea what it was, but it grabbed my attention. For all I could tell from where I was standing, it could have been a piece of glass of some kind, or a piece of metal.

I looked at the shinny object for a moment or two before I decided to retrieve it. I carefully stepped over the remains of a wall of the lodge and worked my way toward the object. I was careful not to step on something that would cause me to fall. When I got to the object, I reached down and picked it up. Holding it in front of me, I examined it. I brushed off as much of the soot and dirt as I could. It looked like a brass plate and handle like one might find on a dresser drawer. My first thought was that it was probably all that remained of all those expensive antiques Neil had stored at the lodge. I decided to show it Monica.

I climbed back over the charred logs, then walked back to the cabin. As I came up to the porch, Monica stepped outside.

"Be quiet, Susan finally cried herself to sleep."

"Good. Maybe she will be a little more willing to talk to us if she gets some rest."

"What do you have there?" Monica asked as she looked at the object in my hand.

"It is about all that is left of the antique furniture Neil had stored in the lodge." I said as I showed it to her.

She took it out of my hand and looked at it closely. She then looked at me and smiled.

"This is a drawer pull, and it is not an antique," she said. "This is from a rather inexpensive chest of drawers that can be purchased at almost any big box store."

"You're kidding."

"No. This is not from an antique. Where did you fine it?"

"I found it in the remains of the lodge."

I thought about what I had just said and what Monica had said. It didn't seem to me that a person like Neil with his love for nice things would have that kind of dresser in his home. I could see if he had just a simple cabin, but the lodge had been over four thousand square feet in size by the looks of the area the remains covered.

"Are you thinking what I'm thinking?" Monica asked.

"Do you think that there might be a case of fraud here?" I asked.

"Based on Neil's reputation, I wouldn't think he would do something like that," Monica said, but not with a lot of conviction.

"I wonder what caused the fire, or if it was ever determined. I think a visit to the insurance company that held the coverage on the lodge and its contents is in order."

"How are you going to find out what insurance company had the coverage? I don't think it would be a good idea to ask Neil," Monica said.

"You're probably right. But I would think the fire department that came to the fire might have it listed in their records. The fire department would have filed a claim for services in putting out the fire. I'm sure that the State Fire Marshal might have that information, too."

"Do you think the local fire chief would give you that information?"

"He might if he thought we were investigating the fire. If we are lucky, he might even have a list of everything that was reported to be in the house as well. It would include the antiques," I said.

"Where do we start?" Monica asked.

"We start with the fire department that responded to the fire. I saw a fire station in Windsor. My guess would be the Volunteer Fire Department out of Windsor responded. If they were not the ones to respond, I'm sure they would know who did."

"What do we do with Susan?" Monica asked.

"I'll have to think about it. For now, just keep an eye on her. We don't want to lose her again."

"Are you getting hungry?"

"Yes."

"I'll fix us something for lunch." Monica said then went back into the cabin.

I walked down the road to where we had left the car and brought it to the garage. I parked it inside the garage so that it would be harder to see. I had no idea if James would return or not. Once I had the car hidden away, I went back to the cabin and sat on the porch to think, and to keep an eye out for trouble.

CHAPTER FOURTEEN

I wasn't sure what I should do about Susan. My first thought was to keep her here with Monica while I went into Windsor to find the fire chief of the local fire department. I didn't think it was such a great idea. There was no way for me to know if James might return while I was gone. To leave Monica all alone with no way to protect herself was just plain stupid.

My next thought was to contact the local fire chief by phone and see if he could come to the lodge. I had no idea what he might be able to tell me. The fact that we had a drawer pull from the remains of the lodge fire, and the fact it was not an antique might get him to contact the State Fire Marshal for me. I was sure that the State Fire Marshal would be interested since there was supposed to be nothing but antique furniture in the lodge. Then there was the possibility the State Fire Marshal would blow it off since we had only found one item that was not an antique. I could only hope he would be interested enough to look into it.

I went inside the cabin just as Monica was putting lunch on the table. Susan had hobbled up to the table and had sat down.

"How's your ankle feeling," I asked.

"A little better," she replied as she looked at me. "What's going to happen to me now?"

"I really don't know. We need to find some place to hide you where you will be safe until we find out what is really going on," Monica said as she set a skillet of vegetables and meat on the table.

"We want to talk to the State Fire Marshal about the fire. We think that it might have been set," I said.

The look on Susan's face gave me the impression that she knew the fire had been set. I didn't know if she had any idea why or who might have set it.

"Susan, do you know why the fire was set?"

"No," she said sharply.

I knew she was lying to me, but I didn't know what she might do if I confronted her with her lie. I also thought she still didn't trust us enough to tell us what really happened here. I decided that it might be best if we gave her a little more time to think about it while we ate lunch.

Monica served up lunch. I could tell by the way Susan looked at us that she wasn't sure how much or what she should tell us. It had been pounded into her for almost four years that Neil was trying to kill her. She had said James was the one who had told her it was Neil who wanted her dead. That got me to thinking.

What was James's reason for telling her that Neil wanted her dead? We had no hint that Neil cared about Susan at all. In fact, Neil had never mentioned her except when I ask him about William's girlfriend. As far as I knew from reports, she had been in California when William had disappeared. I didn't believe it, but all the reports pointed to that conclusion.

There was a very good chance James had helped William hide, but did his involvement go further than that? He seemed to be helping Susan stay hidden. What possible reason could he have for keeping her isolated from the rest of the world? What was he afraid she might say to the authorities? Those were just a couple of the questions I needed answered.

"Susan, if you could go anywhere you wanted to go, where would you like to go?"

Monica looked at me as if she didn't understand where I was going with my question. I wasn't sure what I would get for an answer, but I thought it might get her to start talking to us. It might even get her to tell us something that would be helpful.

"I don't know," she said as she looked at me.

"I understand you have family in California, somewhere around San Diego. Is that right?"

"Yes."

"Would you like to go there?"

"No."

"Why? It would be far from here."

"James said it would be the first place they would look for me."

"Can you tell me who 'they' are?"

She looked at me as if I should know who "they" were.

"Just who are 'they'?" I asked.

"I don't know. James never told me."

I looked at Monica and saw her looking at me. I wasn't sure what was going on in her mind, but I had some serious thoughts about James. It was almost as if he had brainwashed Susan into believing she was in danger if she left the cabin or went anywhere without him. Why would he do that? What was he hiding? What was his part in what had happened?

"If we wanted to take you some place we were sure you would be safe, would you go with us?" Monica asked.

"NO! I can't go anywhere without James," she said in almost a panic.

Susan jumped up from the table and ran to the bed. She laid on the bed and curled up in a fetal position and covered her face with her hands. She began to cry.

Monica looked at me, then went to Susan's side. She sat down on the edge of the bed and gently rubbed Susan's shoulder and back. I got up and left the cabin. I figured it was best if I was not in the room right now. I sat down on the steps of the porch to think.

It was beginning to look like James had done a pretty good job on Susan. She was totally convinced that James was the only one she could trust. Over the years, he had made her totally dependent on him. If I had to guess, when William failed to return from his visit to see his father, James began planting in Susan's mind the idea that Neil wanted her dead.

There was no doubt in my mind that we were not going to get anything out of her, and it would be very difficult if we tried to take her any place where she would be safe. It was looking like it would have to be a place where she was safe from James. The sad thing to me was it would probably take a long time of very careful treatments to get her to trust anyone again.

It was time for me to make a call to the local fire department. Since I didn't have a phone book for the number, I had to go back inside the cabin. As I stepped inside, I could see Monica lying on the bed holding Susan. I looked around and found an old telephone book on a shelf under a small table. I took the book outside and sat down. After looking up the number for the fire department in Windsor, I placed a call on my cell phone.

"Windsor Fire Department, where's the fire?

"There's no fire. My name is Nick McCord. I would like to talk to the fire chief if that is possible."

"That would be Walter over at the Standard station," the woman said. "Is there something I can do for you?"

"I really need to talk to him."

"If you hang on just a minute, I'll get him for you."

"I'll wait, and thank you," I said.

"Just a minute," she said, then I heard the phone being set down.

I didn't have long to wait before a man with a deep voice came on the line.

"This is Chief Walter Morris. How can I help you?"

"Chief, my name is Nick McCord. I'm out at the Cox lodge."

"Yes, Mr. McCord. We met at the gas station. What can I do for you?" he asked interrupting me.

"I understand you were here when the lodge burned down. Is that right?" I asked.

"Yes. I was there when the place burned down. I'm the fire chief. I arrived on the first truck on the scene."

"I was wondering if you could come out here? I found something that I think you will find very interesting."

"Who are you, Mr. McCord?"

"I'm an investigator."

"I'll be there as soon as I can," he said, then the phone went dead.

I closed my cell phone, then smiled to myself. I had a feeling that I was about to open up a can of worms, and I had no idea what was going to come out. I was sure it would open up a whole new investigation into the fire at the lodge. Even if it did open up a new investigation, I still had no idea what it would prove.

I sat and looked out at the remains of the lodge from the front porch of the cabin. I wondered what the fire chief would think when he saw the drawer pull I found in the ashes. My main concern was if he would believe me when I tell him where I found it. The most I was hoping for was for him to get the State Fire Marshal to sent out a fire investigator to dig around in the rubble.

It was only about twenty minutes before I heard a vehicle coming up the road. I stood up and waited for the vehicle to come closer. The first vehicle to come into sight was a bright red pickup with a light bar on the roof. He had no more then pulled up in front of the cabin when a state police car came into view. I had not expected him to bring the police with him, but it might prove to be helpful.

I stepped off the porch and walked out to meet Walter as the police car pulled in behind the pickup.

"Thanks for coming so quickly," I said. "I'm Nick McCord."

"Walter Morris," he said. "I believe you have something to show me that you think is important?"

"Yes. I'll get it."

I returned to the cabin and retrieved the drawer pull. I took it out and handed it to Walter.

"What's up Walter," the state trooper asked.

"Hank, this is Nick McCord. He's an investigator. Mr. McCord, this is Sergeant Hank Berman. He's the local post commander of the state police."

"Nice to meet you, officer," I said as I reached out to shake his hand.

"What do you have there?" Hank asked Walter.

"It's a drawer pull that I found in the rubble of the burned out lodge," I said.

"What's a drawer pull?" Walter asked.

"It's a handle, often made of metal and is found on the front of a dresser drawer. It's used to pull the drawer open," I said.

"You found it in the rubble of the lodge?"

"Yes."

"It would be my guess that there would be several of them in the rubble. There were several dressers in the lodge. It had seven bedrooms," Walter said.

"Yes. I'm sure you are right."

"You had us come all the way out here for this?" Hank said as if he was not too happy with me.

"Walter, were you ever in the lodge before it burned down?"

"Yes, of course. A good many times. Why?"

"Had you ever been in any of the bedrooms?"

"Sure. I was given a tour of the lodge by Neil Cox. I was in every room in the lodge."

"What was the furniture like?"

"The place was full of antique furniture. There was nothing cheap about Neil's furnishings."

"Based on what you saw in the Cox lodge, would you expect to find relatively cheap pieces of furniture in the lodge?" I asked.

"Well, no. I never saw anything in the lodge other than antiques."

"The drawer pull you are holding in your hand is from a rather cheap dresser and is probably not more than about ten to fifteen years old at best. It is certainly not an antique" I said.

Hank looked at the drawer pull Walter was holding. He then looked up at me.

"Are you some kind of an expert on antiques," Hank asked politely.

"No, he is not," Monica said as she stepped out onto the porch. "But I am."

"This is my partner and wife. She is an expert on antiques. The drawer pull is not an antique."

"So what are you saying, Mr. McCord?" Walter asked.

"I think it would be a good idea if the State Fire Marshal would send out a fire investigator and sift through the rubble of the lodge," I said as Monica went back into the cabin to keep an eye on Susan. "If I'm correct, the fire investigator will find nothing in the rubble to indicate that there were any antiques in the lodge when it burned down."

"From what you're saying, you think Neil removed all the antiques from the lodge before he set it on fire? That's a pretty strong accusation."

"I'm not accusing anyone of anything. What I'm saying is, someone removed all the antiques from the lodge before it was set on fire. I have no proof Neil removed the antiques, or that he set the lodge on fire. If he did do it, then he filed a fraudulent insurance claim."

"Maybe, I should go have a little talk with Mr. Cox," Hank said.

"I'm only an investigator - ." I said, but was interrupted before I could finish.

"Don't be so modest, Mr. McCord. You are Detective Nicholas McCord of the Milwaukee Police Department, and an expert on preserving evidence at a crime scene. I remember meeting you at one of your seminars in Milwaukee on that very subject. It took me a few minutes to remember who you are."

"I'm no longer with the police department. I'm a private investigator now."

"Well, I don't know about Walter, but I'm willing to listen to you," Hank said. "What were you going to say?"

"There's more to this than fraud."

My comment quickly drew their attention. I noticed Walter look at Hank.

"I was hired by Neil Cox to find his son. The more I get into the investigation, the more I wonder what is really going on."

"Okay. What can I do to help you?"

"Right now, I would like you to get a fire investigator from the State Fire Marshal's Office out here to go through the rubble of the lodge. I especially want him to be looking for evidence that there were antiques in the lodge when it burned, and evidence that it was arson. I'm sure I don't have to tell him what to look for."

"If he finds there were no antiques, what then?" Hank asked. "There would have to be an investigation by the State Insurance Examiner. Mr. Cox would certainly find out about it then."

"I'm sure he would, but that can't be helped. I just don't want him finding out about it before the fire investigator completes his investigation."

"I don't think that would be much of a problem," Walter said.

"If it is possible, I would like the results of the fire investigator's finding slowed down a little if he finds the kind of evidence I believe he will find. I would also like to know what they find before Neil is told."

"I'll get in touch with the fire investigator for this area as soon as possible. I'll fill him in on what you found and what I knew about the lodge," Walter said, then shook my hand and headed to his truck.

As soon as Walter had left, I pulled Hank off away from the cabin. I didn't want Susan to hear what I had to tell him. I told him about our encounter with Susan and James McPherson at their family's cabin near Athol. I also told him about what took place when we arrived at the cabin on the Cox property, and how we came to have Susan with us.

"Do I need to get someone out here to keep an eye on the place?"

"I think Monica and I will be staying here tonight. We still have a lot to do, but we can spend a night here. Hopefully, the fire investigator will be out here by then."

"I'll see about getting an officer to come out tomorrow night to protect any possible evidence," Hank said. "I'll be back in the morning."

"Thanks. By the way, we don't have any idea if James will be coming back. Do you have a gun you could leave with me? I would like to have some kind of fire power just in case he decides to get nasty."

"Sure. I'll get it out of my car."

Hank went to his car and popped the trunk. He had his head in his trunk for a couple of minutes before he shut the trunk lid. He walked up to me and handed me a .38 caliber revolver.

"It's loaded. It should stop anyone who decides to take you on," he said with a smile.

"Thanks. I'll make sure you get it back," I said as I shook his hand.

"I'm not worried about it," he said. "I best be going."

"Thanks again," I said.

I watched him as he went back to his car and got in. He turned around and drove down the road, disappearing around the corner beyond the trees. I walked back up to the porch then sat down. I had no idea if James would try to come back or not. He would be a fool to try to return, but I kind of wished he would. I would like to have him alone to question him.

I hadn't been sitting on the porch very long after the state trooper left when Monica came out of the cabin and sat down next to me.

"What do we do now?" Monica asked.

"We are going to stay here for the night."

"We're going to have to keep an eye on Susan. I'm afraid she might try to run if we give her the chance. Her sprained ankle won't keep her from trying."

"I'm sure you're right. The state trooper said he would have another officer come out tomorrow to talk with Susan. I would guess that she will be taken to a hospital where she can be confined while being evaluated and treated in the hope of getting her back to normal."

"That would be good. It will keep her away from James. She is sure that William is dead, but it might help if we can prove it. It might help her deal with the reality of it," Monica said.

"I'm sure you're right."

"I'd better get back in there. If she wakes up, I want to be there for her. She needs that kind of security right now."

"I'm sure she does," I said as I watched Monica get up and go into the cabin.

I leaned back and looked up at the sky. It looked like it was going to be a nice night with clear skies and cool temperatures. Since it was still early enough for there to be a couple of hours of daylight left, I thought I would take a little walk around the lodge. I had no idea what I was looking for, nor did I expect to find anything. I just wanted to look around and think.

CHAPTER FIFTEEN

I walked over to where the lodge had been. I spent the next little while slowly walking around the outside edge of what was left of the lodge while looking it over. The damage seemed to be almost total. There were a few of the thicker logs from the outside wall that had not completely burned up. It was clear it had burned very hot as there were very few logs that would even give a person an idea of what had once been there.

From the look of the remains, it seemed that the fire had completely consumed the entire building. With the size of the lodge, it was hard for me to believe it would have burned so completely. There was a fire station less than four miles from the lodge. It would have had to have been almost completely involved before the fire department could get there. That could be explained if there was no one on the grounds at the time of the fire to report it.

Since I had not seen the fire investigator's report on the fire, I had no way of knowing what really happened. I could only speculate as to the cause of the fire. It was an old building which might have contributed to it burning quickly, but from what I understood about it, the lodge had been in very good shape.

As I walked along what appeared to be the back of the lodge, I noticed there was what looked like the remains of a large stove. There was also what looked like it might have been where the backdoor had been located. Part of a small porch was still standing, a couple of steps and a very short section of railing. I got the impression that the area of the lodge I was looking at was the kitchen. I wondered if the fire had started there.

I walked over to the remains of the porch and just stood there looking at it. In among the charred ruins I noticed a small purple flower where I assumed the kitchen had been. I couldn't help but think about the little flower. It was so pretty in among the black, ugly, twisted and charred ruins of the lodge. I moved closer to the flower and knelt down to get a better look at it. I even thought about picking it and giving it to Monica, but decided to leave it there. It was the only thing that seemed to give any hint of life to the blackened remains of what had once been a beautiful hunting lodge.

As I started to stand up, I noticed a can under the remains of the back porch. What caught my attention was its shape. Although it was bent and twisted, it looked like a typical one gallon metal gas can. I just looked at it for a moment or two. I wondered if the fire investigator had seen it. It would be impossible to see from almost anywhere else except from where I was kneeling. I decided it would not be a good idea to remove it. I would let it lay there and tell the fire investigator about it when he got there.

The gas can caused me to think that someone might have set the lodge on fire, but what was the reason? I could think of only one reason based on the information I had received from all of the sources Monica and I had examined so far. Everything we had learned so far pointed to collecting the insurance on the thousands of dollars worth of antiques that were supposed to have been destroyed in the fire. There was also the insurance money for the lodge, which I was sure would be a tidy sum in itself.

Assuming I was correct in my thinking that the antiques had been removed, what happened to them? Where were they now? If the antiques had been removed before the fire and replaced with cheap furniture, that was a sure sign of fraud. If it was fraud, and Neil was the one who caused the fire, why did Neil need the money so badly he would go to such extremes to get it?

I knew that I was speculating. What I really needed was more information. I needed to know if the fire had been arson. That would be the best starting point. I also needed to know if the antique furniture had been removed before the fire. If they had been removed, I needed to know if the antiques were a part of the insurance settlement.

If the fire was accidental and there were no antiques in the fire, and no claim for the value of the antiques was filed, then everything I suspected at the moment was worthless. Even if the fire was accidental and the antiques had been removed, I still needed to know if Neil had collected on them. If he did collect the insurance on the antiques, it was still fraud. It would also be nice to know where the antiques had been taken.

All my speculation did was give me a motive for William's disappearance, but only if he knew his father had burned down the lodge to collect the insurance. It still did nothing to help me find him, dead or alive.

I finished my walk around the remains of the lodge and returned to the cabin. Monica was standing in the doorway of the cabin. I walked up to her.

"I saw you walking around the lodge. Did you find anything interesting?" Monica asked.

"Yes, but I won't know if it means anything until I have a talk with the fire investigator."

"What did you find?"

"I found a gas can under the remains of the back porch. I have no idea if it has anything to do with the fire or not. That would be something for the fire investigator to decide."

"It will be dark soon. Why don't you come inside? I've made a pot of coffee," Monica said.

"Sounds good," I said, then followed her inside the cabin.

I could see Susan lying on the only bed in the cabin. She seemed to be sleeping, but I couldn't be sure from across the room.

"I think I'll sleep in front of the door," I whispered to Monica.

"Good idea. I'll sleep on the bed with her. If she gets up, it should wake me."

"How are you doing?"

"Pretty good. You want to sleep first?" Monica asked.

"Okay. Wake me in a couple of hours so you can get some sleep."

Monica leaned over and gave me a kiss. I took a blanket and laid it down in front of the door. I laid down on it and quickly went to sleep.

* * * *

I was sleeping in front of the door when I was awakened by the creaking noise of one of the floor boards in the cabin. Someone was moving around inside the cabin. I opened my eyes and slowly turned my head. It was dark in the cabin, but there was just enough light from the almost full moon shining in a window that I could make out the outline of a woman standing very still. I was sure it was not Monica because she didn't say anything. The only other woman in the cabin was Susan Small.

"Are you planning on going somewhere?" I asked.

Without a word, she ran toward the door. Since I was lying down on the floor in front of the door, she tried to jump over me. I grabbed her by the ankle and she went crashing through the door and fell flat on her face on the porch. I let go of her leg and stood up. I stepped out onto the porch and knelt down beside her.

"That wasn't very smart," I said.

"I can't stay here," she said.

"Why? Monica and I are here to protect you."

"I heard you say the police were coming out here. I can't talk to the police."

"Why?"

"James will find out. He won't like it."

"James isn't going to do anything to you. He is more afraid of us than you are."

"No, he's not," she yelled.

"You saw him leave. He couldn't wait to get out of here. In fact, he was in such a hurry to save his own skin that he left you behind," I said.

"He'll come back for me. He will. I know he will," she cried then buried her face in her hands.

Monica had a lantern in her hand and was standing behind me. I had seen the look on Susan's face. She was scared to death. I just didn't know who she was more afraid of, James or us.

I turned and looked up at Monica as she stepped outside the cabin. She looked down at me. I wasn't sure what she had on her mind, but she didn't say anything. She simply leaned against the door and looked down at Susan.

"Let's get her back inside," I said.

Monica set the lantern on the porch railing, then went to Susan's side. She helped Susan up. Susan continued to cry as Monica led her back to the bed. Once she was lying down, Monica laid down beside her and wrapped her in her arms.

I picked up the lantern and carried it inside the cabin. After setting it down on the table, I blew the flame out, then moved back to the door. I sat down on the floor and leaned up against the door frame. It wasn't long before the cabin was quiet again. I didn't think Susan would try to escape again, at least not tonight.

* * * *

The rest of the night was quiet. Susan did not make another try at escaping. When I looked at the bed, Monica and Susan appeared to be sleeping. I looked out the door of the cabin. I could see the sun shining through the trees. It looked like it was going to be a very nice day. There was very little breeze and the temperature was comfortable. When Monica woke, she got up and fixed breakfast for all of us. She didn't eat much of it. She said her stomach was a little queasy. It caused me to worry a little about her, but she assured me it was normal and that she would be fine. After breakfast, I went and sat out on the porch.

The sun had only been up for a couple of hours when I heard a vehicle coming toward the cabin. Since I could not see it, I stood up and reached into my pocket. I took the gun that State Trooper Hank had loaned me out of my pocket and held it down at my side while I waited for the vehicle to come into sight.

As soon as I saw it was a state police car, I slipped the gun back into my pocket and stepped off the porch. I could see that it was Hank, but he had another person in the car. It looked like a woman. It made sense because he said he would have another officer come out to the cabin. It only made sense that it would be a woman officer since we were holding Susan.

As soon as the car stopped, I walked over to it. Hank and the woman got out of the car. The woman was wearing the uniform of a state trooper, but she was not carrying a gun. I found that interesting.

"Everything go okay last night?" Hank asked as he walked up to me.

"She tried to run away, but she didn't get off the porch," I replied, then looked at the woman trooper.

"This is Alicia Hoffman. She is one of our auxiliary officers we call on when we need a woman."

"Nice to meet you," I said as I reached out and shook her hand.

Just then Monica came out of the cabin. She stepped off the porch and smiled as she walked toward us.

"This is my wife and partner, Monica," I said.

"It is nice to meet you both," Alicia said with a smile. "I understand you have a woman that is to be taken in?"

"Yes. I'll warn you that she is not very cooperative. She will try to escape if you give her half a chance," Monica said. "She is scared to death that everyone is out to kill her."

"Do you know why she is so scared of everyone?" Alicia asked, her concern showing on her face.

"Not really, but we have a good idea. First of all, it is important for you to know that she has been hiding out for the past five years. For the first year or so, it was with her boyfriend. For the past almost four years her only contact with people has been a guy by the name of James MacPherson. He has convinced her that she is only safe with him."

"Why was she hiding out in the first place?"

"That's a bit complicated," I said. "Right now I think it would be a good idea if we got her into the police car so she can't try to run again. Then we can explain everything," I said.

Alicia and Monica went into the cabin to get Susan, while Hank and I waited outside. It seemed that all hell broke lose inside the cabin. We could hear Susan screaming at Alicia, and we heard the crashing of what sounded like dishes breaking. Hank turned and ran inside. I was right behind him.

Once inside, we saw Alicia had Susan pinned down on the bed. Monica was standing off to the side. She was holding her hand. I immediately went to Monica.

"Hank, I need your cuffs," Alicia called out.

I stood by Monica and watched as Hank moved up next to Alicia and took his handcuffs off his belt. He then put them on Susan, cuffing her hands behind her back. Once she was cuffed, Hank and Alicia forcibly took Susan outside and put her in the back seat of the police car.

While they were outside, I looked at Monica's left hand. It had a small cut on it, but I got the feeling that it was more than that.

"What happened?" I asked.

"Susan threw a glass at me. I blocked it with my left hand and it broke, cutting my hand."

"Let's go over to the sink."

I led Monica to the sink and helped her wash the cut on her hand. I noticed that the back of her hand was swollen and appeared to be bruised. I examined her hand. It hurt her, but I wasn't sure if there were any broken bones. A trip to a doctor would show the extent of the injury.

"It looks like you might have broken a bone in your hand. I'll take you to a doctor and have your hand checked out."

"What about the fire investigator? Isn't he coming out here?"

"I don't know for sure."

"Got a problem," Hank said as he walked into the cabin.

"Susan tossed a glass at Monica. She might have a broken bone in her hand," I said.

"There's a clinic in Dalton."

"Do you know if the fire investigator will be coming out this way?"

"I talked to him on the phone yesterday. He said the local fire chief had called him. He said it would be about noon before he could get here."

"I'm taking Monica into the clinic. If we are not back by noon, will you be able to be here?" I asked.

"Sure. We'll take Susan to the hospital in Pittsfield where they can care for her and keep her safe. I'll have them put a hold on her so no one can check her out or even visit her," Hank said.

"Good," I said.

"We're ready to go. You can follow us," Hank said. "We'll be going right past the clinic in Dalton. They should be able to help."

Monica and I got in the car and pulled out of the garage. Hank had his car turned around and was waiting for us. As soon as we pulled in behind him, he started on down the road that led to the highway.

We followed him all the way to Dalton. He pointed out the clinic then drove on. I pulled into the parking lot of the clinic. Once I was parked, I led Monica into the clinic.

CHAPTER SIXTEEN

It didn't take long for Monica to be seen by the doctor in the small clinic. She had her hand x-rayed. The x-ray showed that she had a small hairline facture in one of the bones in her left hand. The doctor used a hand splint with an ace bandage to hold her hand in place and as a reminder for her not to use her hand any more than necessary. The doctor gave Monica a prescription for pain medication, but she refused it because she thought she might be pregnant.

As soon as she was finished with the doctor, I paid the bill and we left. We immediately headed back to the cabin. We arrived back at the cabin well before noon. There was no one around when we arrived. We went into the cabin and sat down at the table.

"I'm sorry," she said looking up at me.

"What are you sorry about? It wasn't your fault. Just relax. I'll fix us something for lunch."

I found some soup and bread in the cabinet next to the stove. I also found the makings for cheese sandwiches to go with the soup. I started making the soup and sandwiches while Monica laid down on the bed to rest. Lunch was just about ready when I heard a vehicle coming up the road. I turned and looked at Monica. She was awake.

"Would you watch the soup, please? I think we have company," I said as I started toward the door.

As I walked to the door, I took the gun out of my pocket. I checked it to make sure it was ready to use. I noticed there were two vehicles coming toward the cabin. The first one was a bright red pickup with a light bar on the roof from the Windsor Volunteer Fire Department. It was driven by the fire chief I had talked the day before.

The second vehicle was also a bright red vehicle, but it was a larger truck with a light bar on top. On the back was a box with a lot of compartments. It was a truck from the State Fire Marshal's Office.

I slipped the gun back in my pocket and stepped off the porch to greet them. Walter was the first one to walk up to me. He had a smile on his face.

"I see you escorted the fire investigator out here," I said.

"Sure did. He seems real interested in what you found," he said as the fire investigator walked up to us.

"Mr. McCord, this is Larry Chambers, the fire investigator for this area from the State Fire Marshal's Office," Walter said.

"Nice to meet you," I said as I shook his hand. "Please call me Nick. Were you the investigator for this fire?"

"Yes. I understand you have something that you think will be of interest to me."

"Yes. I'll get it," I said, then turned toward the cabin.

As I took a step toward the cabin, Monica came out with the drawer pull I had found. She reached out and handed it to me.

"This is my wife and partner. It might interest you to know that she is an expert on antiques."

"Nice to meet you, Ma'am," Chambers said as he touched the brim of his hat.

Monica smiled slightly then nodded her head to acknowledge the introduction.

"This is what I found in the rubble of the lodge," I said as I handed the drawer pull to him.

He took it and looked at it very carefully. I watched him for his reaction to the drawer pull. He turned and looked at Monica for a second.

"I don't mean to question your expertise, Ma'am, but this is hardly reason enough for me to reopen the investigation of the fire here," Chambers said with a hint of superiority in his voice.

"Did Mr. Cox file an insurance claim for the antiques that were supposed to have been destroyed in the fire?" I asked.

"Yes, he did."

"As you can see, this drawer pull is not an antique."

"That may be so, but there are two problems here," Chambers said, but stopped and turned to see who was coming up the road.

I could see over his shoulder. The car coming toward the cabin was a state police car. It was Hank, a state trooper, returning from Pittsfield. We all waited for Hank to join us.

"As I was saying, there are two problems with me reopening the investigation of the fire. The first is, I don't know where this drawer pull came from. I don't know if it came from the fire here or from some other fire. The only thing I can say for sure is it had been in a fire."

"Chambers, do you know who you are talking to?" Hank asked sharply, but continued without giving Chambers a chance to answer him.

"Mr. McCord is a very well-known and respected expert on collecting and preserving evidence from a crime scene."

"I'm interested in knowing what your second reason is," I said just a little unhappy with Chambers last comment and his attitude.

"There is no reason to believe that the contents of the house were not as Mr. Cox claimed."

"I take it you talked to Mr. Cox about the contents of the lodge?"

"Yes, I did. He gave me a list of the antique furniture that was in the lodge when it burned."

"Do you have a copy of that list with you?"

"No."

"And you accepted the list as proof there were antiques in the lodge?" I asked a little surprised that he would take someone's word for what was in the house.

"Yes. Mr. Cox is very well-known and respected in appraising antique furniture," Chambers said with a hint of sharpness in his voice.

"My brief investigation of the rubble of the lodge indicates that you should have dug a little deeper to establish if the antique furniture that was claimed on the insurance was, in fact, in this lodge when it went up in smoke."

"Just what has your investigation shown you?" Chambers asked, with a hint of arrogance.

Chambers looked like he was a little upset, maybe a little pissed off with me for questioning his ability to do his job. To be honest, that was exactly what I was doing. I believed he had been sloppy and had not done his job the way it should have been done.

"First of all, the fire chief told me that he had been in the lodge only a short time before the fire. He said there was nothing but antique furniture in the lodge," I said.

"That's right," Walter said. "I never saw any furniture that was not antique, and I had had a tour of the lodge only a couple of weeks before the fire. But Mr. McCord found some indication that there was cheap furniture in the lodge when it burned. Like I said, it was a couple of weeks before the fire."

"Did you bother to talk to the fire chief, Walter, about the lodge, or even ask him if he had ever been in the lodge more recently?" I asked.

"I didn't see any reason to question him any further," Chambers said.

"I understand your questioning the drawer pull, but I can show you where I found it. By the way did you find the gas can under the back porch?"

"No," Chambers said softly as the expression on his face quickly changed.

"I did, and it had been in the fire. By the way, it is still there. I didn't move it," I said.

"I'm still not sure there is a reason to reopen the investigation. In fact, I have no intentions of reopening the investigation on the word of someone who has no experience in investigating fires," Chambers said with a note of finality in his voice.

"First of all, you have no idea what my experiences are. But since you are refusing to even consider the evidence, then how about this. If you don't reopen the investigation, I will notify the insurance company that the investigation was incomplete at best. I will tell them that the fire investigator failed to completely examine the remains of the fire for proof that the antiques were actually destroyed in the fire. And what do you think they will do about that?" I asked as I looked him right in the eyes.

I could see that the fire investigator was not very happy with me. I could also see by the look in his eyes he wondered if I would contact the insurance company.

"I think you best reopen your investigation into the fire and its' contents. And I suggest you do it now," Hank said with a hint of authority in his voice.

Chambers looked at Hank. If Hank reported him to the State Fire Marshal and told him that Chambers had done a sloppy job of investigating the fire at the lodge, and he refused to reopen the investigation when new evidence was provided; it could mean his suspension. It might even mean the loss of his job. It would cause a new investigation of the fire that would be done by someone else who would go through every inch of the building. It could prove very quickly that Chambers was incompetent.

"I'll get started," Chambers said with a note of defeat in his voice.

"Good decision," Hank said. "Might I suggest that any drawer pulls or other furniture hardware, such as hinges and knobs that may have survived the fire, be shown to Mrs. McCord for her opinion as to whether they are antiques or junk."

The fire investigator didn't comment. He simply nodded then went to his truck. He drove it over close to the remains of the lodge. Hank and Walter stood next to me and watched as Chambers got his boots and gloves on and began picking around in the rubble of the lodge. They noticed he started at one corner of the remains of the lodge and began to systemically work his way across the rubble. It was obvious that it was going to take him a long time to cover the entire area.

"Gentlemen, the soup is hot and the sandwiches are ready. Would any of you care to have something to eat?" Monica asked. "Will Mr. Chambers be joining us for lunch?"

"We would be happy to join you for lunch. I seriously doubt Mr. Chambers feels much like having lunch right now," Hank said with a grin. "I hope you don't mind, but I told him to bring any drawer pulls or other furniture parts he finds to you to look at. I would like your opinion if they are antique or junk."

"I don't mind at all," Monica said. "I would be happy to look at them."

Monica smiled as she looked at Chambers digging around in the rubble, then turned and went inside for lunch. She put a plate of sandwiches on the table and a bowl of soup in front of each of the men.

"It's very nice of you to fix lunch for us. Thank you," Walter said.

"Yeah, thank you," Hank added.

"You are welcome," Monica said as she sat down to eat with them.

"What do you think Chambers will find?" Walter asked me.

"I have a feeling he will find that there were no antiques in the lodge when it burned," I said. "And maybe he will find it was arson."

"You're expecting a lot, don't you think?" Hank asked. "It's been five years."

"I haven't gotten a list of the furniture that was supposed to have been in the fire. However, I still think there was a lot of very expensive furniture that has just disappeared."

"So you don't really know?" Hank asked.

"To be honest, no, I don't. What I have to do is get a list of the antique furniture that was listed as being in the lodge when it burned. Once I have that and Monica looks over what Chambers finds, I will know for sure if we have a case of fraud."

"You're playing a hunch," Hank said with a grin.

"Yes, but I'm pretty sure I'm right. If I'm wrong, I don't think Chambers would be out there right now. He would have told me to go to hell and left. The fact he is out there digging around for evidence tells me he didn't do his job the first time, and he knows it."

"I've got to hand it to you, you're one gutsy guy. How did you figure out that he didn't do the job right the first time?" Walter asked.

"The gas can. If he had done his job right in the first place, the gas can would not have still been there. He would have taken it to his lab for testing to see if it had been used in the fire."

"I'm sure the Chief Fire Marshal would like to know that one of his men didn't do his job," Hank said. "I think I'll give him a call, but not until we see what he finds this time."

"I think it would be a good idea," I said. "I would hope you will keep it quiet for a few days. I still need to check with the insurance company on what was claimed and what was paid out. I don't want Neil Cox to get wind of what is going on here."

"We won't say anything, will we Hank."

"Not until we have some real solid evidence that a crime has been committed," Hank said.

"Fair enough," I said.

"I should be getting out there and do my job," Hank said as he stood up. "Thanks for the lunch. Give me a call if I can be of help."

"I will," I said as I shook his hand. "And thanks for your help."

Hank nodded. We watched him as he walked out of the cabin and went to his car. Before he drove off, he took a minute to look out at Chambers and smiled.

"I figured I'd stick around for a little while to see if he finds anything," Walter said. "After all, it is fire department business."

"That will be fine with us," Monica said. "Would you like a cup of coffee?"

"I sure would."

"I'll have it ready in a few minutes."

Walter thanked Monica for lunch, then left the cabin. I asked Monica to sit down while I made a pot of coffee.

"Do you really think Chambers is going to find anything," Monica asked.

"I sure hope so. If he doesn't, I will look a little foolish. It wouldn't be the first time."

"He looks like he is working hard to find something," she said as she looked out the window toward the remains of the lodge.

"Nick, what do we do next?" Monica asked with the sound of worry in her voice.

"Once we find out there is no evidence of any antique furniture having been destroyed in the fire, we need to find out the name of the insurance company that insured the furniture. Then we have to find out if a claim was made on it. All we have so far is what we have been told, that being he had filed a claim. We don't have any proof."

"Isn't all this about the fire leading us away from finding William or what happened to him?" she asked.

"I don't think so. I think there is a connection between the fire and William's disappearance. I've got a feeling that the secret Susan would not tell us was that William knew that his father collected on a fraudulent claim. He may have known why his father did it."

"I guess I don't see it."

"The date of the fire, and the date when William began having trouble with the law, pretty much coincide. It could mean that the fire had really upset William. Why, I don't know.

"About four or five months after the fire, William disappears. We know from Koato that William was struck by his father just before he disappeared. We also know from some of the investigators that Neil didn't seem to want his son found. That tells me something is going on here and all the evidence points to Neil having something to do with it.

"Then there's James MacPherson. He also has something to do with it, but I have no idea what. He is in it up to his neck."

"I guess I see your point, but we don't have any real proof, nor do we have any idea what happened to William," Monica said, concern showing on her face.

"And there in lies the problem."

"I guess we have to find some proof," she said with a grin.

"Correct," I said.

"How do we go about that?"

"I'm hoping some proof comes from the remains of the lodge."

I stood at the window and watched Chambers as he sifted through the rubble. Walter was leaning against the fire investigator's truck watching Chambers, as well. I thought I saw Chambers pick up something and put it in a small plastic bag. I wondered if it was something we could use to prove our theory was correct.

"Nick, the coffee is ready. Would you like to take a cup out to Walter," she said as she handed me a cup of coffee.

"Sure."

I waited for her to hand me another cup, then walked out to the remains of the lodge. When I got there Walter looked at me and the coffee, then smiled.

"Thanks," he said as he took one of the cups.

I turned my attention on Chambers. He seemed to be very much interested in one small area. I took a minute to look around the remains, then turned my attention back to Chambers.

"Do you think he found something?" I asked Walter.

"I think he is working in the area of the master bedroom. It looks like he might have found something. Let's just wait and see."

We waited for several minutes before Chambers turned around and saw us watching him. He turned back and began picking up several small items from the rubble. I was unable to see what they were, but I was sure it was important. Chambers straightened up and began walking toward us. He had several items in a plastic bag.

"You might want to show these to your wife," Chambers said as he handed me the plastic bag.

I took them from him, then asked, "What do you think you found?"

"If I'm not mistaken, those are hardware off some bedroom furniture."

"I'll take them to her," I said as I started to turn to go back to the cabin.

"She might want to rinse them off so she can get a better look at them."

"I'll tell her."

"It would be nice if you would bring me a cup of coffee. It looks like I will be here for awhile," Chambers said politely.

"Would you like a sandwich?"

"That would be nice. Yes."

I walked back to the cabin and gave the bag to Monica. After telling her what Chambers had said, I got a cup of coffee and a sandwich, then took them out to him. He seemed to appreciate it. I returned to the cabin to see what Monica had in the bag.

When I got back to the cabin, Monica was just finishing rinsing off the contents of the bag. She had them laid out on a towel next to the sink. She turned and looked at me with a big smile.

"These are pieces of hardware from furniture in a bedroom. None of them are from antiques," she said.

"I think we have what we need here."

"What about the rest of the lodge?"

"I think he will be continuing his search for more pieces of furniture hardware."

I left the cabin and retuned to the remains of the lodge. Walter looked at me as I approached. I could see that he was waiting for me to tell him what Monica thought of Chambers findings.

"None of what Chambers found are from antiques."

"What now?" Walter asked.

"Can you keep an eye on Chambers? I want to make sure he completes the investigation of the fire this time."

"Sure. What are you going to do?"

"I think it is time for Monica and me to go talk to a couple of people about what we found."

"Okay. What do you want me to do when Chambers is finished?"

"Nothing. When he is done, let him go where he wants, but you keep the evidence so Monica can look at it. I'll give you my cell phone number just in case something comes up you think might be important," I said as I gave him one of my cards.

"Okay. I'll hang on to the evidence in case you need it."

"Thank you. Do you happen to know the name of the insurance company that had the policy on this place?"

"Not offhand, but I have one of the claims representative's cards back at my office. Stop by the fire house. I'll call ahead and have one of the firemen give it to you. I also have one from the insurance appraiser. They both gave me cards in case I needed to get in touch with them."

"Great. Thanks for all your help. I think we better get on our way. We still have a lot to do."

"Keep in touch," Walter said as he shook my hand.

"I will," I said then returned to the cabin.

Monica and I packed up our belongings and the evidence Chambers had given us. We got in the car and left.

CHAPTER SEVENTEEN

Once we got out on the highway, we headed for the Windsor Fire Department. When we arrived, there was a fireman leaning against the door frame. Behind him was a big yellow firetruck with a big chrome siren on the front bumper. He straightened up as we pulled in, and walked toward us. As he approached the car, I rolled down the window.

"Are you Mr. McCord," he asked.

"Yes."

"Walter told me to give you these cards."

He handed me two business cards through the window. I immediately glanced at them then handed them to Monica. After thanking him, I backed out onto the street and headed toward Northampton where we would pick up Interstate 91 and go south.

"Did you look at these cards?" Monica asked.

"Not really. I just checked to see if there were two of them."

"The claims representative named on this card is James MacPherson," she said as she looked at me for my reaction.

"Why am I not surprised. I think that explains a lot, don't you?"

"Yes, I do," she said.

"We might have a hard time getting a list of the antique furniture that should have been in the house when it went up in smoke."

"It sure would be nice to have it," she said, then sat looking out the car window.

I glanced over at her. I wondered if her hand might be uncomfortable or even hurting a little as she was holding her injured hand in her other hand. But she also looked like she was thinking about something. I decided not to disturb her thoughts, but instead gave her a chance to finish them. It was only a short time before she looked at me and smiled.

"Nick?"

"Yeah."

"We have what amounts to a house full of antique furniture that is missing. Right?

"Yeah."

"The lodge was a pretty good size building, and according to Walter the lodge was full of antique furniture. If the furniture was not in the lodge when it burned down, then where was it?"

"I don't know," I said. "What are you getting at?"

"I think all the furniture from the lodge was moved to the Cox Estate," she said, her voice showing she was convinced she was right in what she believed.

I didn't respond to her comment right away. I had to think about it. The house was certainly big enough to put them in. The fact we had not seen all the furniture that was in the house made me wonder if Monica might be right. Although some people might think it was not a good place to hide the furniture, I couldn't help but think that it was the perfect place. If he mixed the furniture from the lodge with the antique furniture already in the house, who would know? It would be hidden in plain sight.

Another thought hit me. He had the perfect place to get rid of the furniture, too. If he had taken it to his store in the city, he could sell it off a piece at a time and no one would be the wiser. There was also the fact that no one would think twice about a truckload of furniture being delivered to the store. It probably happened several times a month.

Another thought crossed my mind. Even if we had a list of the furniture, it might not do us any good. It had been five years since the fire. If he had removed the furniture before the fire, he could have sold it all off by now. It would be very hard to prove what he sold was the same furniture.

"I'm afraid you may have hit on something. The problem is the fire was five years ago. In the five years since the fire he could have sold it all off, or at least a good part of it."

"I hadn't thought about that," Monica said with the sound of disappointment in her voice.

"Don't be too upset with yourself," I said. "He may not have sold off the furniture and still has it at his home. He might have been afraid to sell it for fear that someone would be watching him to see if he did. After all, many criminals get caught because they sell off what they stole and end up leaving a paper trail.

"Like who? I mean, like who would be watching him?" Monica asked.

"An insurance investigator, either hired by the insurance company or one of their own investigators. The insurance company might wonder why he kept so much antique furniture in a lodge where no one was living a good part of the year."

"Wouldn't the insurance company tell James since James was the claim representative?" Monica asked.

"They might, but not if they knew that James was a friend of William, or if they found out James grew up right next door to the Cox family."

"Even if Neil did keep the furniture for fear that someone would discover he still had it, we don't have a list of the all the furniture that was in the lodge when he was showing it to the fire chief," Monica said.

"I think you hit on something. The fire chief had probably gotten a tour of the house so that someone not closely associated with Cox could verify the furniture was there. The problem I have is we don't have a list of what was in the lodge, and we haven't seen the furniture in the rest of the house on the estate."

"True. Think about this. If Neil doesn't know we have been to the lodge, he might give us a tour of the rest of his house," Monica said. "If you will remember, Mia suggested to Neil that he give us a tour of the house since I'm interested in antiques."

"What about James? Don't you think he would tell Neil we had been at the lodge?"

I could see Monica thinking about what I had said. Even having said it, I had no proof that James and Neil were involved in anything together. I had a feeling they were, but I couldn't prove it.

Then there was the fact that Susan Small had been under the control of James for the past four years. What was that all about? Did Neil know James was keeping Susan in hiding? Did Neil know about Susan staying at the cabin next to the lodge? All good questions, but no good answers.

"I don't know," I said in answer to Monica's question. "One thing we could find out, and probably should, is did James ever return to work at the insurance company," I said. "Remember, he left his office in one hell of a hurry."

"Yes, he did. The next time we saw him, he was with Susan at his family's cabin near Athol. Why was he hiding Susan?"

"I don't know, but think about this. James might actually be in love with Susan, but with his involvement with Neil, he couldn't let it be known that she was still in the area," I suggested as a reason for him to be protecting her.

Another thought had occurred to me was how was he able to keep her a secret for so long while still working at the insurance company? I managed to come up with an answer, but I was not sure if it was the right one. He might have been able to keep Susan a secret if his claim area was in the western or northern part of the State of Massachusetts. I had heard of guys that travel a lot having two families in different parts of the state. Apparently not a real common practice, but it did happen from time to time. He didn't have two families, but why couldn't he be caring for Susan and staying with her while checking claims in western or northern Massachusetts? I was sure that he would have to spend some time in the office; but as a claim's representative, I would think he would travel a great deal of the time in his assigned area. That was something I would have to check out.

Monica and I didn't have much to say for sometime. I think we were both caught up in our thoughts. The miles passed by quickly. We were at the junction of Interstate 91 and highway 9. I turned onto Interstate 91 and headed south. It wasn't very long and we crossed into Connecticut again. As we were passing through Hartford, I remembered there was a PI in Glastonbury that we wanted to talk to.

"Monica, what was the name of the PI we wanted to talk to in Glastonbury?"

"Give me a minute and I'll look it up."

Monica reached into the back seat of the car and grabbed the folder with the names of all the investigators who had worked on the case. It didn't take her but a minute or so to find his name and address.

"Norman Picklock," she said with a grin. "I wonder if his name has anything to do with what he does."

"Are you sure that's right?" I asked.

"I'm sure. I have his address and his phone number right here."

"Why don't you call him before we get too close to Glastonbury? See if we can meet with him."

"Okay."

Monica picked up her cell phone and placed a call to the number she had for Mr. Picklock. He must have answered fairly quickly. I could only hear Monica's side of the conversation, but it was clear he could see us as soon as we got to his office. Monica jotted down the directions to his office, then hung up.

Monica gave me the directions. We turned off on Highway 2 and headed southeast. It wasn't long and we were at Glastonbury. Monica navigated me right to the address we had for Mr. Picklock. I pulled into the parking lot alongside the four-story building. We got out of the car and walked into the building. There was a directory next to the elevators. I found Mr. Picklock had his office on the third floor. We took the elevator to the third floor and got off. It only took a couple of seconds for me to figure out where his office was likely to be. We started down the hall to the left.

When we got to his office door, I knocked on the door and waited. It was only a moment before a rather short stocky man opened the door. He smiled at us, especially Monica.

"Come in," he said as he stepped back so we could enter.

"I'm Nick McCord and this is my wife and partner, Monica," I said as he shut the door.

"I'm glad to meet you. Please, have a seat."

We sat down on the chairs in front of his desk while he walked around and sat down behind the desk.

"What is it I can do for you?"

"As Monica had explained on the phone, we are looking into the disappearance of William J. Cox."

"That case is a sore spot for me, but how can I help you?"

"Why is it a sore spot for you?"

"That damn Cox. Oh, excuse me, Ma'am."

"That's quite all right. You are not the only one who feels that way about him," Monica said.

Mr. Picklock looked at Monica then turned and looked at me. I got the feeling he knew we had talked to at least some of the other investigators who had worked on the case.

"Mr. Cox fired me just when things seemed to be leading me in the right direction. If I could have solved the case, it would have been a real feather in my hat, so to speak."

"So you thought you were getting close?"

"I don't know if it was getting close, but I thought I was making some very good headway. I had found out that Susan Small was in Massachusetts. Now, I wasn't able to find out where, but it was in the northern part of the state, probably in some cabin on a lake. There are a lot of cabins and hunting lodges in the northern part of the state."

"Interesting. What happened?" I asked.

"I told Cox that Susan Small might have returned from California. That was where everyone I had talked to told me she had gone. If she had gone, she had come back. Anyway, I told him I was going to check it out."

"How were you going to check it out if you didn't know where in northern Massachusetts she was hiding?"

"I had a hunch that she was staying at the MacPherson's cabin somewhere close to Athol. I figured it wouldn't be too hard to find someone who knew where the cabin was located."

"I see. Did you ever find out if she was there?"

"No. The minute I told him that I thought she might be there; and I was going up that way to see if I could find her, he fired me. He gave me a big check and told me I was done."

"Did he give you a reason?"

"He said that he had spent enough money and was sure his son was dead. He said there was no need to continue to waste money looking for him."

"How long after William disappeared did Neil hire you?"

"He had been missing for just a little over four years. If you've seen the report I gave Mr. Cox, you already know that."

"Yes, I do. What I'm looking for is anything you might have found that you didn't report, or any hunches you might have had or a lead that you didn't get a chance to follow up on."

"Nothing really. I had thoughts about Mr. Cox and what he was doing. I wondered if he was really trying to find his son, or was he just putting on a show for someone. Maybe, for his wife?"

"We have had the same thoughts."

"Then why did you take on the case?"

"Because after looking at all the reports and information, we think something is amiss here."

"He'll probably fire you before you get very close to the answers," Mr. Picklock warned.

"He might, but we plan to find the answers anyway."

A smile came over his face. I got the impression that he was sure we would do what we said.

"I wish you luck. If you can use my help, I'll help out," he said with a grin.

"Thanks for the offer, but right now about all the help you can be is to let us know if you can think of anything that might help us," I said as I stood and handed him my card. "You can call us at this number."

"You got it," he said as I stood up and reached across the desk. "I'll go over my reports and see if it brings anything to mind."

We shook hands with him, then left his office. I didn't say anything to Monica until we were on the elevator.

"What do you think of him?" I asked.

"I think he was honest with us. I'm sure he meant it when he said it was a "sore spot" for him."

"I think he was being straight forward with us," I said.

"Where to now?" Monica asked as we left the building.

"It's getting kind of late. Our next PI is located in New London, I think."

"Yes, he is."

"How about we drive onto Knollwood's Resort and Casino for the night? It will be pretty late by the time we get there."

"We can have a late dinner there," Monica suggested.

"Okay, Knollwood's it is."

We left the parking lot. I headed for highway 2 that would take us toward Norwich. It was only a few miles from Norwich to Knollwood's Resort and Casino.

* * * *

We arrived at the Knollwood's shortly after nine. I figured there was no sense trying to contact Sam. He would surely have gone home. We checked in, then went to one of the restaurants for dinner. When we were finished, we went directly to our room.

It didn't take us long to get out of our clothes and into the shower. We didn't take very long showering, we were tired. Neither of us had gotten very much sleep the night before. We curled up together and quickly went to sleep.

CHAPTER EIGHTEEN

We woke to the sound of the phone ringing next to the bed. I looked at the clock on the bedside table. It was seven-thirty. With our late arrival it seemed a little early for us to get up. I reached over and picked up the phone.

"Hello," I said, still half a sleep.

"Nick?"

"Yeah.

"Sam here. I hope I didn't wake you."

"You did, but it's okay. What's on your mind?"

"I was wondering how things have been going. Are you any closer to finding out what happened to William?"

"I'm afraid not. Say, did you know Neil had a lodge up near Windsor Massachusetts?"

"No. I didn't know that. I didn't know Neil had a lodge anywhere."

I was a little surprised by his statement. I would have thought that Sam would have known about the lodge since Sam had told us they were good friends.

"He did, and it burned down about four or five months before William disappeared."

"Really? He never mentioned it to me. What kind of a lodge was it?" Sam asked.

"A very big one. It was a hunting and fishing lodge for the very wealthy at one time."

"I didn't know anything about it. I take it you have checked it out. It would seem to me it would have been the perfect place for William to hide out if he didn't want to be found. But since it burned down before he disappeared, that kind of lets it out as a place to hide."

"Yes, it does do that," I said.

"Since you are here, do you have something else you wanted me to help you with, or are you just stopping off on your way to somewhere else? I noticed you got in pretty late."

"We have a PI in New London we want to talk to this morning. After that, I think we will return to Long Island. I would take it as a personal favor if you would not say anything about what we said here to Neil," I said.

"Sure. I take it you found out something you don't want Neil to know?"

"Yes, at least for now. It could jeopardize my investigation, and cause a problem for us. I need time to check it out to make sure what I believe is correct. To say anything more now could prove to be counter productive."

"You've got my word. I won't say anything to anyone about our conversation. Will you let me know how things work out when you are done?"

"Sure."

"Okay. Is there anything I can do for you?"

"No. I don't believe so."

"In that case, how about letting me buy you breakfast since I woke you up?"

"Sure. How about meeting in the Veranda Café in – say – thirty minutes?"

"Sounds good. See you there," he said then hung up.

I turned and looked over at Monica. She was looking at me.

"How are you feeling this morning?"

"Pretty good. I'm a little hungry."

"In that case, how about getting dressed so we can have breakfast with Sam?"

"Okay," she said, then rolled out of bed.

Monica went into the bathroom while I got dressed. She looked a little pale when she came out.

"You okay?"

"Yes. I'll feel better when I get something in my stomach."

I nodded that I understood, but I really didn't. I knew women went through morning sickness to different degrees of discomfort. Monica seemed to be handling it pretty well. I once again thought about taking her back home, but I knew she wouldn't go for it.

It was only a little while before she was ready to go to the Veranda Café for breakfast. We left the room and began walking toward the elevator. I took hold of her hand and she looked up at me and smiled.

It was only a few minutes before we arrived at the Veranda Café. We told the hostess who we were there to see. She said that Sam was already there, then led us to his table. Sam stood up until Monica was seated.

"It is good to see you again," Sam said. "I won't get into a discussion on your investigation since we talked a little about it earlier."

"I do have a couple of questions that might help if you don't mind?"

"Not at all. What do you want to know?"

"Do you know that Susan Small never went to California?"

"No, I didn't know that. I believe I told you she never picked up her last check."

"You did. There is some question as to whether she ever left the east coast."

"So her parents lied about her leaving," Sam said.

"It seems so. She is currently in a hospital under protective custody by the police."

"What's wrong with her?"

"Physically, nothing other than a sprained ankle she got when she tried to get away from us."

"I take it from your statement there is something mentally wrong with her?"

"Yes. We think she has been, for the lack of a better word, brainwashed. The guy we saw on your tapes with the fancy belt buckle was James MacPherson. James was a friend of William."

"I remember seeing him on the tapes, but I didn't know he was William's friend," Sam said.

"Have you seen him here since William disappeared?"

"No, but that doesn't mean he hasn't been here. Do I need to keep an eye for him?"

"I don't think so, but it wouldn't hurt. I don't want you to do anything about him, but watch him and let me know," I said.

"You got it."

"By the way, I take it you still have Susan's check?"

"Sure."

"Hang onto it. She might need it when she gets out of the hospital."

"No problem. Would you let her know that we are holding it for her?" Sam asked.

"Sure."

We finished our breakfast while talking about nothing related to our case. We then said our goodbyes to Sam. After checking out of our room, we went to our car and left Knollwood's Resort and Casino for New London.

* * * *

It didn't take us very long to find where the last PI we wanted to talk to had his office. It was located on the sixth floor of a downtown office building. It overlooked the Thames River.

We parked in the parking lot and walked into the building. We found the elevator and took it to the sixth floor. It didn't take but a couple of minutes for us to find the office. We entered the outer office where we were greeted by a woman in her mid-forties. As we walked up to the woman's desk, I could see through the partially opened door.

There was a man who looked to be in his early forties sitting at a desk.

"May I help you?" the woman asked.

"Yes. We would like to speak to Mr. Michael Murdock, if we may?"

"Can I tell him what it is about?"

"I'm Nick McCord and this is my wife and partner, Monica. We would like to talk to him about a case he worked on about three years ago. He had been hired to find William Cox."

"Margaret, I'll talk to them," the man in the office called out to her.

"Please, go in," she said politely.

As we entered the office, the man stood up. He looked like he was in pretty good shape. He was wearing a dark blue suit with a white shirt and a red stripped tie. There was a slight bulge on the left side of his suit coat. It was clear that he was carrying a gun in a shoulder holster.

The office was nicely decorated and had a great view of the river. The desk was very large and was made of solid oak. There were a couple of oak chairs in front of the desk with dark brown leather seats and backs. He pointed to the chairs for us to sit down.

"Please, sit down. What is it I can do for you?" he said very politely.

"I'm Nick McCord, and this is my wife and partner, Monica."

"It is nice to meet you. I'm Mike Murdock. What is it you would like to know about William's case?" he said getting right to the point.

"First of all, we have talked to several of the private investigators who worked on the case. We have been especially interested in those who seemed to be making some headway then were suddenly discharged, like you. Can you tell us why you were discharged by Mr. Cox?"

"I like a man who gets right to the point. To answer your question, I don't have the foggiest idea why I was fired. One day I was working for him, the next day I was fired."

"Your last report to Mr. Cox indicated that you believed Susan Small had not gone to California. Can you tell us what brought you to that conclusion?"

"Sure. I checked out every mode of public transportation that she could have taken to get to California and found nothing. The only way she could have gotten to California was to walk or drive. She didn't have a car and I checked for credit cards, but she didn't have any. I checked out William's credit cards but there were no charges on them after the day he disappeared. She just plain dropped out of sight. I had a feeling she was hiding somewhere, probably with William," he said.

"Did you know that Neil Cox had a hunting lodge in Massachusetts?"

"No, I didn't know that. But William's friend and neighbor had a cabin near Athol, Massachusetts. I also found out James MacPherson and William Cox would often go there during the summer, and had been going there for many years. It made sense that he might have been hiding there, but I found no evidence of it," Mike said.

"Then you found the MacPherson cabin?"

"That would be correct. It's not an easy place to find," he said with a slight grin.

"How long did you work on the case?"

"I worked on it for about – ah – five months."

"From the reports you gave Mr. Cox, you made some very good progress for such a short time," I said.

"I sure think I did, but I guess Cox didn't think so. I will say this, though, he paid me well. He even gave me a bonus when he fired me."

"Didn't it seem a little strange that he would give you a bonus when he fired you?"

"It did, but I wasn't going to turn it down. I worked hard to find out as much as I did."

"I'm sure you did. What are your thoughts about the case? You know, things you thought or had a feeling about, but couldn't prove."

"To be honest with you, I got a very strong feeling that Mr. Cox didn't want his son found. It was almost as if he was putting on a show for the rest of the world. You get my drift?"

"I sure do. Several of the other PIs we have talked to have said pretty much the same thing."

"If you have seen the reports from the PIs Cox has hired and fired, why are you interested in being another PI that he has run around the country for a little while and then fires?" he asked.

"You know Mike, I've asked myself that very same question."

"Did you come up with an answer?" he asked with a chuckle in his voice.

"I have. We have decided to make every effort to find out what happened to William, with or without Neil Cox's approval. In short, he can fire us, but he can't stop us from looking for William."

"I take it he doesn't know how you feel?"

"That would be correct."

"It could get very expensive for you, if he fires you."

"A friend of ours told Mr. Cox that we were good, but expensive. If we are fired, he will find out just how expensive we really are," I said with a big grin.

Mike looked at me for a minute, then began to laugh. We had found out as much as we were going to find out from Mike. It was time for us to leave. Monica and I stood up.

Mike stood up and reached across the desk. I reached out and shook his hand.

"It was nice meeting you. I wish you all the luck in the world," Mike said.

"Thank you for your time. If we are ever in the area again, we'll look you up."

"You do that. Would you do me a favor?" Mike asked.

"If I can."

"Let me know how it ends. I would like to know that someone found William. I would also like to know what you find out."

"I can do that," I said.

Monica shook his hand, then we turned and left. He was still standing behind his desk when we walked out the door.

It didn't take us long to get to the car. Once we were in the car, I sat looking out the windshield.

"What's on your mind?" Monica asked.

"We have been getting pretty much the same answers from the PIs we've talked to about Cox. They all think that he is putting on a show. They don't think he is really looking for his son. It seems to be that way from the first PI he hired to the last. We have believed that way after only a day or so of looking at the reports. So far I have not seen anything to make us change our minds. None of them think he is really looking for his son."

I continued to sit there thinking about what we had found out from the PIs, and what we found out about the lodge. I couldn't help but think that Susan and James knew the answers. The problem was Susan was in the mental ward of a hospital, which would make anything she said suspect. As for James, he had disappeared, and we knew him to be a liar.

I turned and looked at Monica. She was watching me.

"What now?"

"I think I would like to call the fire investigator and see what he found. And when we talk to him, I want to ask him if he can get a list of the furniture Cox claimed was in the lodge when it burned."

"Do you think he will give it to us?"

"I think so. He knows he's in a lot of trouble with Walter and Hank, especially if either of them decides to report him to the State Fire Marshal. I would think that he would want to be as cooperative as possible."

"We don't have a phone number for the fire investigator."

"Call Walter at Windsor. He should have a number for him."

Monica looked up the number then placed a call on her cell phone. She put the phone on speaker so I could hear what was said.

"Windsor Fire Department.

"Hello. This is Monica McCord. I would like to speak to Walter if I may."

"Sure. He's standing right here."

I could hear her tell Walter he had a call from a woman.

"Hello?"

"Walter, this is Monica McCord."

"Oh, Hi, Monica. What can I do for you?"

"We are trying to get a list of the antique furniture Neil claimed was in the lodge when it burned. Do you happen to have the phone number for the fire investigator? I'm sure he has a copy."

"I think I have a copy of it. I got it from the appraiser of the damage to the lodge and its contents. I could send you a copy," Walter said.

"That would be great. Do you have a fax machine there?"

"Sure do."

"I'll have to call you and tell you where to send it. We are on the road at the moment. I don't want it sent until we are there to get it."

"I understand. By the way, I'll send you a copy of the fire investigator's report. But for your information, he didn't find anything to indicate there had been any antique furniture in the lodge when it burned. In fact, he said that there was very little furniture in the lodge for the size of it. Your husband was right. He found very few parts to any kind of furniture. It looks like they didn't even try to replace all the furniture with cheap stuff before it burned. He also thinks that there is a strong possibility it was arson, but with the delay in doing the job he should have done the first time he was at the lodge, he lost a lot of evidence that it was arson."

"Did the fire investigator send a copy of his findings to the insurance company?" I asked.

"No. I convinced him that it was in his best interest to keep it as quiet as possible for at least a couple of days. The fire investigator gave me a copy of his report, and he said he had written it to indicate there was evidence enough to make him want to reopen his investigation."

"Very nice, Walter."

"I hope it helps," Walter said.

"I'm sure it will. I'll call you when we are ready for the list and the report. Thanks so much for your help," Monica said.

"You're welcome," Walter said then hung up.

Monica looked over and smiled. We had what we needed, and it looked like we might get the time we needed to see if the antique furniture was in the house at the Cox estate. I had no idea what our next move would be if we didn't find it there.

I reached down and turned the ignition key to start the car. The car started and I drove out of the parking lot. I got on Interstate 95 and headed for New York City.

CHAPTER NINETEEN

It was late in the afternoon when we arrived back at the Cox Estate. We were immediately let in through the gate and drove up to the house. As I passed through the gate, it occurred to me I might want to talk to the guard. I thought I would do that on one of our walks to "stretch our legs".

We no more than stopped in front when Koato came outside. He walked down the steps and greeted us at the car. He reached out and politely opened the door for Monica.

"Welcome back," he said. "Mr. Cox is home. He has been waiting impatiently for your return."

"Oh, really," Monica said, then glanced my way.

"Yes, ma'am."

"Tell me something, Koato. Does Mr. Cox appear to be rather nervous?" I asked.

Koato gave no indication that he thought my question was at all strange. However, he hesitated to answer. I wasn't sure, but I thought I saw a hint of a smile on Koato's face. I got the impression he was pleased that Neil was feeling a bit nervous. I could not think of one reason that he should be pleased, unless he believed that my question made him think I had reason to believe Neil should be nervous. Koato looked at me for a moment before he spoke.

"Yes. Does he have reason to be nervous?"

"I'm not sure, but I'll bet we will find out soon enough," I said with a slight smile.

Just then Neil stepped out onto the porch. He did look a little nervous, but tried to put a smile on his face. I noticed that the look on Koato's face turned serious.

"Welcome back," Neil said. "I hope your trip was fruitful."

"I'm not sure. We are expecting some information to come in. We'll have to wait and see what is in the information to know for sure."

"Does it look promising?"

"Like I said, we'll have to wait and see."

"Well, come in. Dinner will be ready shortly."

While Koato took our luggage to our room, we followed Neil into the den. Neil sat down in a chair near the windows. Monica and I sat down in chairs facing him.

"Tell me about your trip. I figure it is going to cost me a pretty penny, as they say," he said with a grin that looked more forced than natural.

"It isn't going to cost you all that much."

"Tell me about it. What did you find out?"

"Well, it wasn't all that exciting. We talked with Sam again at Knollwood's Resort and Casino." I said.

"What did he have to say?"

"He said to say 'Hi', to you. Other than that he really didn't have anything to add to what he told us before. I do have a question for you, though."

"Okay. What is it?"

"Can you tell me how close your son was with Susan Small?"

"I don't understand what you are asking."

Neil looked a little confused. The expression on his face showed some concern over my question.

"Well, it seems that several of the investigators you had hired were told that she left for the west coast at least a couple of months before William disappeared. Do you think that she left and he was to join her later, say a month or so later?"

I watched Neil for some kind of a reaction. All he did was stare at me. I thought I could see in his face a hint of interest in why I would ask such a question. It was almost as if my question caused him to wonder what we might have found out.

"I guess, I don't know. It is possible," he said.

I was sure my question had set him back. It was not one he was expecting, nor was he prepared to answer it.

"Do you think he went to California?" Neil asked.

"No. In fact, I'm pretty sure that he didn't. I'm also pretty sure Susan didn't go to California, either."

Now that brought a reaction. I got the impression that he was sure she was out of the picture, but he now had some doubts. I also got the feeling he knew she had not gone to California.

"I – ah – I thought she had gone to California to stay with some of her family," Neil said.

My question and comment had obviously caused Neil some concern. I wasn't sure if it was because of what Susan might know and tell if she was found, or if it was because he thought we might have already found her.

"There is something else that bothers us a little."

"What might that be?" he asked as if he really didn't want to hear the question.

"We have been going over all the reports - - - -," I started to say but was interrupted by Koato.

"Excuse me, but dinner is ready, sir. Mrs. Cox is already at the table."

"I guess your question will have to wait. I don't like to keep Mia waiting. She tires easily these days."

Neil immediately stood up and started toward the dining room. I looked over at Monica and smiled as I stood up. It was very clear that I had rattled Neil a bit, which was my plan. It was clear that he was going to use the delay to think about what he should say. Monica had picked up on what I was doing. She reached out, took hold of my hand and gave it a light squeeze.

We followed Neil into the dining room. Mia was sitting in her wheelchair on one side of the long table near the end. Neil had walked to the end of the table. I walked with Monica to the side of the table that would put me next to Neil and Monica next to me. It also put Mia on the opposite side of the table directly across from me.

Once we were all seated, the dinner was brought in from the kitchen. Nothing was said for sometime. It seemed that Neil had little interest in talking at the moment. He was not going to continue our discussion in front of Mia. In fact, the first person to speak was Mia.

"Monica, did Neil ever get a chance to show you around the house. He has some very interesting antiques upstairs?"

"No, not yet. We have been a little busy, but I would certainly be interested in seeing some of his antiques. The ones in the guest room are absolutely beautiful."

"Neil, you must show them around," she said with a smile. "He has so many antiques in the upper levels of the house. Some of them are very old and very beautiful.

"You will show her around, won't you Neil," Mia said as she spoke directly to him.

Mia looked at Neil as if she was insisting on him showing Monica the rest of the antiques in the house. I wondered why she was so insistent on it. Did she know something or was it just the way she handled him.

"Certainly," Neil said, then turned and looked at Monica. "We could do that right after dinner, if you would like."

I got the feeling Neil was not one bit interested in showing Monica the rest of the house and the antiques in it. He was probably more interested in not talking to me until he had a chance to think. His smile at Monica appeared to be forced.

"That would be nice," Monica said.

"Mr. McCord, how was your trip these past couple of days?" Mia asked.

"I guess the best I could say was it was interesting."

"Did you find out anything that will help you in your quest to find my son?" Mia asked.

I'm not sure what it was, but there was something in the way Mia talked and looked that gave the impression she was being much more forceful than she had been in the past. The last time we talked, she talked about "their son", this time it was about "her son". I don't know why I picked up on that, but I did.

"I'm afraid nothing all that helpful. However, we did get a little better picture of what might have happened. Mostly, it was just verifying some of the information that we found in the reports we have been looking over."

"Does that really help you any?"

"I would have to say, yes. Mostly it helped us understand your son a little better. By knowing him, we might be able to figure out what was going on in his mind when he disappeared."

"I can see where that might be important," Mia said. "Did you get any new leads that might help you find him?"

"Not really. We think William may have spent sometime at the MacPherson's cabin near Athol, Massachusetts. The problem is there is no way of knowing how long he was there."

"Why would he go there?" Mia asked.

"I don't know, but a police report we received from the Massachusetts State Police showed that William had been stopped for speeding near Athol while driving James's car. The report indicated James was in the car with William."

"Really? I didn't know about that," Mia said. "Was that in all those reports you were going over?"

"No. I had a friend of mine send out inquires to several of the surrounding states for any information they might have on William. It was in several reports we received from my friend."

I glanced over at Neil. He seemed a little pale. It was my guess he thought we would use only the reports that he had provided.

"What does it mean?" Mia asked.

"We don't know that it means anything. Could you give us some idea of why he was driving James' car when he had a perfectly good car of his own?"

"Mia, I don't want you to get too upset. Maybe we should stop for tonight," Neil suggested.

"I want to know what it means," Mia insisted.

"It simply means he was stopped for speeding. He was probably going up to the MacPherson's cabin with his friend James. He might have been going there to relax and think about whatever was troubling him. We are pretty sure he was troubled about something. It would help if we knew what was troubling him, but we are not likely to find out what that was unless he told someone. Our talk with James didn't get us the answer," I said. "Do you happen to know what was troubling him?"

"No. I wish I had. Maybe I could have kept him from running away," she said with a sad look in her eyes.

"I think that is about enough for tonight," Neil said rather forcefully. "I'm sure Mr. and Mrs. McCord are tired after their trip," Neil said.

"Yes, I think that is a good idea," Monica said. "I would like to have a tour of the rest of the house before I turn in, if you don't mind?"

"That would be fine," Neil said. "Are you coming, Mr. McCord?"

"No. I have a couple of things I would like to look into before I turn in. You and Monica go ahead without me. Besides, she is more interested in antiques than I am," I said with a smile.

I stood up and pulled Monica's chair back so she could stand.

"Mia, I enjoyed having dinner with you," I said.

"Maybe we could talk again tomorrow?" Mia asked.

"I would certainly enjoy that," I said.

"Thank you for a lovely meal," Monica said to Mia.

I followed Monica and Neil out of the dining room. They were talking about antiques. I was thinking about getting the information I needed from Fire Chief Walter. I walked into the room that had been set up for us, sat down in a chair and opened my cell phone. Just as I was ready to punch up Walter's phone number, Koato came into the room. I closed my cell phone and looked up at him.

"What is it, Koato?"

"I was wondering if you would like me to bring in coffee for you?"

I'm not sure what it was, but I got the feeling that Koato wanted to say something to me.

"No, thank you," I said then waited for him to leave or say something.

"Is there something else?"

"No, sir," he said then turned toward the door.

I watched him as he left the room. I wondered what it was he wanted to say. I guess I would just have to wait until he decided he wanted to tell me. I wondered if it had anything to do with the fight that Neil had had with his son the night before William disappeared. Maybe I could find a time and a place where Koato would feel more comfortable in telling me what was on his mind.

I glanced at my watch and decided it might be a little late to call Walter. I turned and looked out the window toward the front lawn. It was at that moment I remembered I wanted to talk to the security guard at the gate. I could see that there was someone still in the guardhouse at the gate. I got up and left the house.

* * * *

I walked across the well manicured lawn to the gate. The guard must have seen me coming toward him because he went back inside the guardhouse then came out a small door that allowed him to come inside the grounds without opening the gate.

"Good Evening," I said as I approached him.

"Good Evening, Mr. McCord. Is there something I can do for you?"

"Yes. I was wondering, is this gate the only way onto the grounds?"

"No, sir. There is a back entrance off the side street over there," he said as he pointed toward where the wall made a sharp turn.

"Is there a guard there, too?"

"Only during the day, usually from seven a.m. to four p.m. He is there to let delivery trucks in and out. All deliveries go through that gate."

"Is the gate locked when there is no guard on duty?"

"Yes, but it is monitored in the front gate house and in the house."

"How would someone get in if he had a late delivery?"

"He would have to come to this gate. If it was a legitimate delivery, he would have to come to the front gate."

"If it wasn't a legitimate delivery?"

"We would not let him in without checking with someone at the house."

"Are you here all the time? Maybe better put, is there someone here around the clock?"

"No, I work the late shift, Monday thru Friday. I come on at four and get off at mid-night, unless there is a party or something that would keep guests coming in or out after midnight. There is a guard who works the morning shift, and two who work the weekends."

"How would someone get in after you have left?"

"There are two ways. They would have to be let in by someone at the house, or they would have to have the code to open the gate."

"Who has the code," I asked.

"Only members of the family and some of the household staff. Koato has the code for sure."

"How long have you been working for Mr. Cox?"

"About three years. I go to school during the day."

"That's good. Thanks for the information. Have a good night."

"You, too, sir."

I turned and headed back toward the house. To get a truck in here with a lot of antiques on it, and without being seen, would have to be done at night. It would have be let in the back entrance by someone in the family or on staff. The only staff member who was here all the time was Koato.

Another thought came to mind. Since Neil was an antique dealer and apparently stored a lot of antiques at his home, why would a truck have to be brought in at night? Neil dealt in antiques all the time. Moving antiques in and out of the house would be nothing unusual. No one would think twice about it.

Well, that idea led me nowhere. The only thing left for me to do was to go back to the house and see if Monica had found out anything.

* * * *

Just as I entered the house, I found Koato standing in the entryway. He always seemed to be there. It was almost as if that was his duty post whenever either Monica or I went outside.

"Good Evening, Koato."

"Good Evening, Sir."

"Have Neil and Monica finished their tour of the house?"

"I don't believe so. Would you like me to find out?"

"No, that won't be necessary. You can tell Monica I'm in the room with all the reports when she is done."

"Yes, sir."

I went into the room Neil had set up for us. I sat down in a chair near the window to think. With all the information we had, I still had no proof that a crime had been committed. I didn't think we were any closer to finding out what happened to William, either.

The only facts we had were that William had disappeared. We had nothing to show if he was alive or dead. No witnesses, no body, no nothing. Even with all the information we had in the form of police reports and PI reports, we still didn't have any idea what had happened to him. Everything we had were speculations, theories and gut feelings, none of which would stand up in court. We didn't even have a clear motive for his disappearance. What we did have were several things that didn't make sense.

Just then Monica came into the room. She had a big smile on her face.

"Neil has some very valuable and rare antique furniture in this house."

"I take it you enjoyed yourself," I said with a smile.

"Very much. I have not seen so many pieces of fine antique furniture in one place in my whole life. The second and third stories of this house are like a museum."

"It's getting late. How about a short walk before we go to bed," I suggested. "You can tell me all about it while we walk."

"That's a good idea," Monica said knowing full well why I wanted to take a walk.

We walked to the front door and left the house. As we stepped out on the well groomed lawn, Monica took my arm and leaned close to me. We walked slowly away from the house.

"You know how all the furniture in our bedroom matches?" Monica asked.

"Sure, you made a point of it the first time we saw the room," I said wondering what she was getting at.

"Almost every room we went into had at least one or two pieces of furniture that didn't go with the majority of the rest of the furniture."

"What are you trying to say?"

"For example. One of the rooms was done in very old and rare French Provincial. There had to have been eight or nine pieces of furniture in room that matched. Yet, in one corner was a tall English styled armoire in a dark walnut and from a completely different time period. If the room had been set up for the French Provincial, the armoire was totally out of place."

"Maybe he didn't have any place else to put it," I suggested.

"True, but maybe he needed a place to put it because he had more furniture in the house than he had places to keep it. Or maybe by spreading out the furniture from the lodge, he hoped no one would notice if they were not all together in the same room."

"That's a very good point. The problem we have is we don't know what was in the lodge."

"You didn't get hold of Walter?" she asked.

"No. I thought it was too late. I'll call him first thing in the morning. If he sends us the list of the furniture that was supposed to be in the lodge, could you tell if the furniture you saw tonight was part of what was claimed to have been in the lodge?"

"Maybe," she said.

"That will have to do until we get the list and the Fire Investigator's report."

"There's one other thing. We didn't go up to the fourth floor of the house," Monica said.

From the look on Monica's face, she was thinking the same thing I was. I wondered what was on the fourth floor.

"Did you ask about it?"

"Yes. He said most of what was up there was just parts of antique furniture."

"That's interesting. If it is parts, could that mean he is using old parts to fix damaged furniture?" I asked.

"If he is doing that, the value of a repaired piece could be considerably less than if the piece had all its original parts," Monica said.

"Do you think he is doing that?"

"I don't know. It would be all right to do it if he didn't claim it was all original. If he is using parts from other furniture to repair a damaged one and tried to pass them off as originals, he could be cheating whoever buys it if the person thinks it is all original."

"If he is passing the repaired ones off as all original, then it would not be too far a step to committing fraud by filing a claim for destroyed antique furniture that was not destroyed." I said.

"The problem we have is proving it," Monica said.

"I would like to get up to the fourth floor of the house and see what is there."

"So would I. We'll have to work on a way to get up there without Neil or anyone else in the house knowing about it. Did you see the way up there?"

"Yes. I also noticed a big lock on the door," Monica said.

"I think we should head back. We should get a good night's sleep. We have a lot to do. I want the list of furniture that was in the lodge before we take the chance of going up to the fourth floor."

"Sounds like a good idea," Monica said.

We turned around and walked back toward the house. When we arrived, Koato was standing just inside the entry way. We greeted him, then told him we were calling it a night. He watched us as we went up the spiral staircase to the second floor.

Once we were in our room, we got ready for bed. Monica curled up against me and laid her head on my shoulder. She was running her hand in small circles over the hair on my chest. I knew she was thinking about something, but I wasn't sure just what it might be.

"I think you will make a great father," she whispered in my ear.

I gave her a gentle squeeze then closed my eyes. It wasn't long before I could tell Monica had drifted off to sleep.

I didn't fall asleep right away. I spent sometime thinking about what she had said. Her comment led me to believe that she was pretty sure she was pregnant. I smiled to myself with the thought of having a little one to raise. It both scared me half to death and excited me at the same time. With the thought of fatherhood on my mind, I drifted off into a peaceful sleep.

CHAPTER TWENTY

I woke early in the morning. Monica was still sleeping. I got up and walked over to the window and sat down on the window bench. Pulling the curtain back just a little, I looked out over the well groomed lawn. The sun had not come up over the tree covered hills, but it was light enough for me to see if anyone was out there. In the early pre-dawn it looked so peaceful and quiet. There were still a few lights on near the front gate and along the street out in front. Once the sun came up, they would go out.

From where I was sitting, I could see all the way down the drive to the guardhouse by the gate. There was nothing moving on the front lawn. I decided it was a good time to let my mind wander over the past few days.

Before I could get my mind settled on our investigation, I noticed a movement near the front gate. I could make out the movements of a man dressed in the blue uniform of the security guards. He stood near the speaker outside the gate and leaned down as if talking into it. Within a few seconds, the gate began to open. It was clear that he was the guard just coming on duty. The guard stepped inside the grounds, then walked to the door at the back of the guardhouse. It took him a couple of seconds to unlock the door before he opened it and went inside. Shortly after he entered the guardhouse, the light came on inside, and the gate closed. Everything was quiet again. The security guard was at his post.

With nothing more to draw my attention outside, my thoughts returned to our investigation. The first thing to enter into my mind was did Neil set his lodge on fire, or did he arrange to have the lodge burned down, or had the fire been accidental. I had no proof that it might have been arson other than the burned gas can I had found under the back porch, and the speculations of the fire investigator. I hoped to get something from the fire investigator that would show what caused the fire. If it turned out to be arson, then the question became who set it and why.

Neil was my top suspect in the fire because he seemed to have the most to gain from the fire, but I couldn't prove it. I knew finding the proof that would answer my questions would be hard since the fire occurred five years ago. Time would make it harder to find proof that the fire was intentional.

Another reason for me to think it was arson was the fact that all the antique furniture had been removed from the lodge just a few days before the fire. Walter, the local fire chief, had told me that he had seen the lodge full of antique furniture when he was given a tour of it just a week or so before the fire. That brought up the question of what happened to the furniture.

I wondered what had become of the furniture. Did Neil sell off the furniture, or did he stash it some place? If he sold it off, it might be hard to prove. If he stashed it, the fourth floor of the house seemed like the perfect place to hide it. There was little chance anyone would accidentally discover it there. There was certainly enough room to store all the furniture that had been in the lodge, and then some.

My thoughts turned to Neil and some of the inconsistencies between what we found out and what he had told us. His firing of the PIs when they were obviously on the right track showed a blatant disregard for the facts, or at least what I considered facts. I had a lot of questions about what was going on. The only conclusion I could come up with for Neil to have fired some of the PIs was he didn't want his son found. That didn't make a lot of sense to me, unless he was trying to hide something. If he was guilty of something, he would have been better off to stop looking for his son years ago. By continuing, he had actually cast suspicion on himself as having something to do with William's disappearance.

My thoughts turned to what Monica had told me last night. If I assumed Neil had nothing but antique parts on the fourth floor of the house, then I wondered if he was repairing and selling furniture that wasn't what it was represented to be? Did he file a fraudulent claim on the furniture not destroyed in the fire? Did the fire have anything to do with the disappearance of his son, William? All were good questions. I wasn't sure what it was going to take to find the answers.

What I did know was we had to be very careful how we found any evidence. If we were able to find proof that Neil had committed a crime, our evidence had to be obtained legally or it would be tossed out of court. I remembered that I had talked to Koato, and he had said Neil and William had had a fight the day before he disappeared. I wondered if Koato would talk to me again if I could get him away from Neil. I also wondered what he might say. I had no idea what he knew, but if anyone knew any of the secrets of this house, he would be the one.

My thoughts turned to William. So far none of the information we had discovered seem to be getting us any closer to finding out what happened to him. My problem was I had it stuck in my mind that everything we knew and everything we thought we knew had a connection to William's disappearance. I just couldn't find the connection. There had to be something out there that would connect all the dots for me.

My thoughts were disturbed by Monica. I turned to look at her. She was beautiful lying in the bed looking at me.

"Good morning," she said with a smile.

"Good morning. Did you sleep well?"

"Yes. Have you been thinking about William?"

"Yes and no. I've been thinking about a lot of things. One thing I'm absolutely sure of is Neil had something to do with William's disappearance. And the fire at the lodge has something to do with it, too."

"I thought you were already sure of that?"

"I am, but now I have no doubt he is involved in William's disappearance. I just don't know how he is involved."

"Okay, how do we find out how he is involved and how do we prove it?"

"We start by getting Neil out of the house."

"That should be simple enough since it is his house," Monica said with a grin. "Just how do you suggest we do that?"

"I'm not sure," I said. "But I will think of something. Right now, I think it would be a good idea if we got dressed and had some breakfast. I have a couple of phone calls to make."

Monica didn't reply to my last statement. She rolled out of bed and went directly to the bathroom.

While she was in the bathroom I got dressed. I then returned to the window seat to wait for her. It wasn't long before she returned to the bedroom. She looked a little pale as she had for the past several mornings. It worried me.

"Are you all right?" I asked.

"Yes," she said with a smile. "My stomach is a little upset, that's all."

I didn't know what to say. There was nothing I could do about it.

"Are you ready to go to breakfast?"

"Yes."

We left the room and started down the hall toward the stairs. I took her hand as we walked down the hall. When we got to the stairs, I looked up toward the third floor.

Although I was looking toward the third floor, I was thinking about the fourth floor. I noticed that the staircase didn't go beyond the third floor.

Monica looked at me. She must have figured out what I was thinking.

"The stairs to the fourth floor are at the end of the third floor hall. Actually, there are stairs at both ends of the third floor hall with doors at the top of the stairs."

"Is there any other way to get to the fourth floor?"

"Not that I know of, but there might be."

"Is there any other way to the third floor from here?"

"Yes. There are narrow stairs at each end of this hall."

"Okay."

We turned and started down the staircase. When we reached the bottom of the spiral staircase, we found Koato standing there. He was watching us come down.

"Good morning," Koato said.

"Good morning," I replied.

"Breakfast is ready in the sunroom. This way, please."

Koato didn't wait for a reply. He simply turned and led us to the back of house where the sunroom was located.

The sunroom was a rather large room with lots of flowers and other plants giving it the air of being outdoors. The backyard was full of flowers and was well groomed like the front yard. Neil and Mia were sitting at a round glass top table. As we entered the room, Neil put his paper down and stood up.

"Good morning," he said.

We both said good morning. Neil directed us to where there were empty chairs. I ended up sitting between Neil and Monica, while Monica was seated between Mia and me.

"I do hope you had a pleasant night," Mia said.

"Yes, we did," Monica replied politely.

"What are your plans for today? More reports to go over?" Neil asked.

"I have a couple of leads I hope to get some information on today," I said.

"Oh. Where are they coming from?"

"One is from a Massachusetts State Fire Investigator," I said as I watched Neil for a reaction.

The look on Neil's face was priceless. He suddenly looked like he had swallowed something that didn't agree with him. It was obvious he didn't expect us to find his burned down lodge.

"What possible information could a fire investigator have that would be relative to your investigation?" Mia asked.

"First, my question. Neil, why did you keep the fire at your lodge a secret?"

"My lodge burned?" Mia asked, then turned to Neil. "Neil!"

"I didn't want to worry you about it," Neil said.

"Why not? It was my father's lodge. It was my lodge," she said sharply.

Now that was a bit of news. Maybe it was time to find out who had the money in this family. It was beginning to look like it was Mia.

"How did you find out?" Neil asked, seeming to have regained his composure.

"It is not important how we found out. What is important is you didn't tell us about it. We told you in the beginning that we needed to know everything, and we expected everyone in the house to be honest with us, including you."

"Mr. McCord, do you think my son might have died in the fire at the lodge?" Mia asked, almost afraid of what we would tell her.

"No," Monica said. "The fire took place at least three or four months before William disappeared."

I was looking at Mia while Monica told her. She seemed relieved that William had not died in the fire. Maybe she was hoping he was still alive.

I turned and looked at Neil. He didn't seem to be so relieved. I got the impression he was still very worried, as he should be. If the information I expected were to arrive, it might prove he had filed a claim and accepted payment for losses that had not occurred in the fire.

"I have to go to the office this morning. I have a very important meeting. When I get back, I expect the two of you to be gone," Neil said in a sharp, commanding voice.

I was not surprised that he had fired us. It seems we were getting just a little too close to something he didn't want us to know.

No one bothered to say anything. We simple watched him stand up and walk out of the sunroom. Almost as soon as he left, Koato came into the room. He walked around behind Mia and very gently put a hand on her shoulder as he stood behind her wheelchair.

I watched Koato closely. He showed a great deal of concern for Mia, more than one would expect from a household staff member. Mia reached up with one hand and put it over Koato's hand. She turned her head and looked up at him, then turned to look at us.

"We have not been totally honest with you, either," Mia said softly.

"No, we haven't," Koato added. "The first thing you should know is William is not Neil's son. He is our son. I am William's father."

I looked at Monica only to find her looking at me. I knew that Koato was very fond of William, now I knew why. I turned back and looked at Koato, but didn't say anything.

"We have been in love with each other since shortly after I first came here," Koato said. "Neil was always away on business, buying and selling antiques. I took care of Mia.

222

I listened to her, cared for her, and fell in love with her. One day, we went a little too far with our love for each other and she became pregnant.

"When Neil found out, he blew up. He insisted that Mia have an abortion, but she refused. He fired me, but Mia told him I was to stay. He threatened to divorce her because she had been unfaithful to him.

"Mia told him that he would not get a penny of her money if he tried, and she would tell the world about the women he was having affairs with in New York City. You see, she had had him followed by a private investigator. She found out he had been unfaithful to her for years, even before I was hired to help her run the house. All those nights he spent in his apartment in New York City were not spent alone.

"Neil never asked for a divorce after that. He knew if he did, he would get nothing; and his reputation would be destroyed. He would not be able to live the lifestyle Mia had provided him. Although his business was doing fairly well, it would not provide him with the lifestyle to which he had grown accustomed."

"You have been living that way ever since?" Monica asked.

"Yes. Neil spends most of his time in New York City. Some of the antiques on the third floor, and all the antiques on the fourth floor belong to Neil. Everything on this floor and the second floor belong to me, plus most of the antiques on the third floor are also mine," Mia said.

"This arrangement actually works out for both of us. There isn't anyone in this community who knows anything about it," Koato said. "We agreed to it in order to avoid a big scandal and to provide William with the advantages he might not otherwise have if everyone knew."

"Did you know that the lodge had a good number of antiques in it?" I asked.

"No. I didn't know that," Mia said. "You see I have not been to the lodge for almost twelve years. I have not been there since the automobile accident that put me in this wheelchair. The wheelchair makes it hard to get around where there are no sidewalks."

"So you knew nothing about them?" Monica asked.

"That's right. If there were antiques in the lodge, they belonged to Neil. All the antiques I had in the lodge when I inherited it were moved here when I couldn't go to the lodge any more," Mia explained.

I looked at Monica. She was looking at me. I could tell that she was wondering where we go from here.

"What are you planning on doing now?" Mia asked.

"As you heard, we have been fired," I said. "But we still have not found out what happened to William."

"Neil may have fired you, but I would like to hire you to complete the task Neil originally hired you to do, that is to find out, for us," Mia said as she patted Koato's hand, "What happened to our son, William. I will be glad to pay all your fees and expenses. I will not put any limits on your activities in your efforts to complete your search for the truth. You may go wherever your leads take you, or wherever you think it is necessary to go to reach your goal."

"Thank you for your vote of confidence, but I can not guarantee you that we will ever find out where William is, or what happened to him. I can only guarantee that we will do the best we can. We will also stop our search for him if we find we cannot complete the task. Is that fair enough?"

"That is fair enough," Mia said with a smile. "I would like to know if you have used up the retainer Neil paid you?"

"Not yet," I said.

"When you do, come see me. I will give you the money to continue your search," Mia said.

"I think it is time for us to make a phone call. I need to know what the fire investigator found in the ruins of the lodge, and get a copy of the list of antiques that were supposed to have been in the lodge when it burned," I said.

"You should have something to eat before you go back to work. I insist you have your breakfast first," Mia said.

"He does work better on a full stomach," Monica said with a slight chuckle.

We had a very good breakfast before we returned to the room we had been working in. As soon as I sat down, I placed a call to Walter in Windsor.

"Windsor Fire Department. Where's the fire?"

"It's me again. No fire."

"Oh. Hi, Mr. McCord. Walter told me you might be calling today."

"Is Walter around?"

"No. He's out at the Lodge, the one that belongs to Mr. Cox."

"What's he doing out there?"

"Some guy from the insurance company came by. He wanted Walter to go out to the lodge and look around with him."

"Do you know the name of the guy?" I asked.

"No, but he has New York license plates on his car."

That caused me to get a little concerned. I wondered if the guy was James MacPherson.

"Have you ever seen the guy from the insurance company before?"

"No. I don't believe so," she said.

Her last comment brought me a sigh of relief. I didn't think James would ask the fire chief where the lodge was located since he had been there not more than a couple of days ago. But if it was James, he may have wanted the fire chief out there to find out what the fire investigator found.

There was also the possibility that the fire investigator had notified the insurance company about his second look at the lodge. If that was the case, the insurance company might have sent out an investigator to find out what was going on.

"Do you know if the fire investigator sent a report of what he found to the insurance company?"

"Yes, he did. Walter told me that he had sent a report to the insurance company. He said you would want one, too, but the insurance guy told me not to send it to you. He doesn't know I kept a copy of the report because Walter said you would want it. I didn't like the guy, besides I don't work for him. I work for Walter," she said with a chuckle.

"I would like you to send it to me along with the list of items that were supposed to be in the lodge when it burned."

"Just give me your fax number and I will get it off to you."

I gave her the fax number, then she left the phone. It was only a moment or so and she was back on the phone.

"They are on their way," she said.

Suddenly the fax machine came on line and started printing. It didn't take long before several pieces of paper were starting to come out of the machine.

"It looks like I'm getting them," I said as I picked up the first couple of pages.

"Good. I hope they help you in your case. I got a feeling someone is responsible for that fire. I would like to see them caught," she said.

"I can assure you that it will help. Thank you for your help. Please don't tell anyone you sent them to me, except Walter, of course. And thank Walter for me."

"I will," she said then hung up.

I took the seven pages of paper from the fax machine, then separated them. I gave the list of items which included the furniture that was supposed to be in the lodge when it burned to Monica. She sat down in a chair and began going over the list.

I took the report of the fire investigator findings, sat down in a chair and began reading it. Listed on the top of the report were the names of those who were to get a copy of it. One was to go to the State Fire Marshal's Office, one to the insurance company claims office, one to the Windsor Fire Department Chief and one to me. I found it interesting the "insurance guy", as he had been called, didn't want me to have a copy. It caused me to think that the "insurance guy" was James MacPherson.

As I began to read the report, I noticed the first couple of sentences gave the reason for the fire investigator to reopen the case. They did include the fact we had found the gas can that was hidden under the rear porch, and the drawer pull we found in the ruins. He admitted he had not done as thorough a job as he should have, and with the new evidence felt he should reexamine the remains of the lodge.

The report went on to tell what he found. The report showed there had not been any antique furniture in the lodge, and what remains of furniture he did find were the remains of relatively cheap everyday furniture one might find in almost any house. The report proved that the antiques Walter had seen in the lodge had been removed.

"We now have proof the antique furniture that was in the lodge had been removed before the fire," I said to Monica.

"That's great. I'm not a hundred percent sure, but I think I have seen the armoire listed here," she said as she held up the lists of items claimed to have been in the lodge.

"Do you think it's the one you saw on the third floor?"

"That very one."

"I think it is time to see if Mia will let us unlock the doors to the fourth floor and take a look around up there," I said. "I also have a few questions to ask her."

"Since all the furniture on the fourth floor belongs to Neil, don't we have to have permission from Neil or a warrant to pick the locks?"

"No. The house belongs to Mia. It is her decision as to where we can go or can't go on the property."

We got up and started out the door. For the first time, Koato was not practically standing outside the door. I looked around and didn't see anyone.

"Where did they go?" I asked.

"My guess is they are together. If I was her, I would want to go out to my garden. It is the one place where she feels at peace"

"Okay. Lead the way"

Monica started off toward the dining room, then on out the backdoor. I simply followed Monica.

CHAPTER TWENTY-ONE

We found Koato and Mia sitting side by side near a small fountain in the center of a beautiful garden. Koato was sitting in a chair next to Mia in her wheelchair. They were holding hands and talking softly to each other. I didn't want to disturb them, but I needed to talk to them.

Excuse me," I said as we walked toward them. "We are sorry to interrupt you."

"It's quite all right, Mr. McCord. What is it?" Mia asked.

"Would it be okay with you if we open the doors to the fourth floor? We want to check out some of the furniture up there."

"Certainly. What do you think you will find up there?"

"I think we might find the antique furniture, or at least some of it, that was supposed to have been destroyed in the fire at the lodge."

"How will you know the furniture is from the lodge?" Mia asked.

"We have a very detailed list of all the furniture that was insured and was supposed to be in the lodge when it burned. The insurance company required it because of its value. Monica is very well qualified to tell if the furniture on the fourth floor is the same furniture," I said with a smile.

"You have my permission to look anywhere you wish. You can even look in my bedroom if you wish," she said with a smile.

"I don't think that will be necessary," Monica said with a smile.

"Thank you. I'm sorry we interrupted you," I said.

"That's all right. Koato and I have a lot of plans to make. Things are going to be different around here."

I didn't bother to ask her how it was going to be different. I simply smiled and took Monica by the hand. We left Koato and Mia in the garden and headed back into the house.

We immediately went up the stairs to the fourth floor. I took a look at the lock on the door. It didn't look like it was going to be too hard to open. I left Monica at the door while I went to the kitchen and asked the cook for a screwdriver. He showed me where a tool box was stored. I took the small tool box and returned to the fourth floor.

When I arrived, I didn't see Monica, but I saw the door was open. I wondered how in the world she got it open. I stepped inside and found Monica looking over a large dresser. She had a drawer out of it and was examining the bottom of it.

"How did you get in?"

"I gave it a sharp pull and it popped open. Not a very good lock," she said with a grin. "By the way, this is one of the pieces of furniture on the lists. If I had to guess, it is one of many of them that are here. He didn't store parts here like he said. He kept up here some of the best examples of English furniture from the seventeenth and eighteenth century and early American furniture that I have ever seen."

"That's great, but is there enough from the list to prove he removed it before the fire?"

"There's enough to prove the furniture was removed from the lodge before the fire, but I'm not sure we can prove he actually removed it."

"The furniture is here, it was his place to store furniture, and he was the only one we know of who had the keys to this part of the house. That's enough to implicate him in its removal from the lodge and probably enough to get a warrant for his arrest."

"That's true enough. What do we do now?" Monica asked.

"I think it's time to bring in the police. Try not to touch any more of the furniture than you have to. Fingerprints may show that Neil had a hand in moving it."

Monica nodded she understood what I was saying.

"I would like you to go through the rooms on this floor and check off each piece of furniture you find that is on the list. I would like to know just how much of it is here."

"What are you going to do?"

"I'm going to call the police and ask them to send out a detective. Then I'm going to alert the guards that they are not to let anyone come into the estate to remove any furniture. I want this evidence secured."

"I'll get started," Monica said.

After I gave Monica a kiss, I turned and left her to inventory the furniture. I returned to the garden where I found Mia and Koato still talking. From what little I heard, they were making plans to live there as husband and wife.

"Excuse me, again," I said as I interrupted them.

"What is it?" Koato asked with a smile.

"I would like to call the police and have them come out here. We found most of the furniture that was supposed to have been in the lodge when it burned. I would like to have a talk with them; but I'm sure once we open the door to what we believe happened, you will have to answer some very pointed questions."

"We have nothing to hide anymore, Mr. McCord," Koato said. "Please do what you think is necessary. Our main concern is finding out what happened to our son. We will cooperate in anyway we can."

I looked past Koato at Mia. She smiled as if she agreed with him.

"I would also like it if the security guards you have on the property would secure the grounds so that no one can remove anything from the house."

"I take it you are referring to Mr. Cox coming on the property and removing some of his furniture?" Koato asked.

"That is correct," I replied. "If he removes the furniture, we might lose some leverage against him. I believe he might know something about William's disappearance."

"I'll notify them immediately."

"It might also be helpful if Mia were to call the police."

Koato and I looked at Mia. She had heard everything we had said.

"I will do that. Koato, would you push me into the den, please."

Koato walked around behind her wheelchair, looked down at her and said, "Gladly, dear."

Koato headed for the den. I followed along behind.

Once inside the den, I walked over to a window and looked out. I could hear Mia calling the guardhouse at the front gate.

"This is Mrs. Cox. I want you to immediately secure the gate and not allow anyone inside except the police. Do you understand?" she said.

There was a moment where she simply listened.

"I mean anyone, and that includes Mr. Cox. You are not to allow him in. Is that clear?"

I didn't hear what the guard said, but it was pretty clear he had responded in the affirmative. She then called the rear gate where deliveries were made and gave them the same instructions. She hung up and looked at me.

"The property should be secure, Mr. McCord."

"Thank you."

"What's going to happen now?" Mia asked.

"That will depend on what the police have to say, and on what Neil does when he can't get his furniture back. It could get a little uncomfortable for you," I said.

"I'll call them now," Mia said, then picked up the phone.

I watched as she called the local police. I heard her ask for a detective. It was a couple of minutes before a detective came on the line.

"Detective Morris, this is Mia Cox. I would like you to come out to my estate. I have a private investigator here who would like to talk to you," she said then listened for a moment or so.

"No. I think you will find what he has to say well worth your trip out here," she said which was followed by a short pause.

"His name is Nicholas McCord. He goes by Nick McCord," then there was another pause.

"Yes. I believe he is from Wisconsin."

Mia looked up at me and smiled.

"Yes, I do believe he is one-and-the same," she said then paused.

"Thank you. I will notify my security guard that you are coming."

Mia looked up at me again as she hung up the phone.

"Mr. McCord, were you a detective with the Milwaukee Police Department?"

"Yes. But please call me, Nick."

"Detective Morris apparently knows you. It seems you are pretty well known in the police community."

"I have been told that before," I said with a grin.

"What now, Nicholas?"

"We wait until Detective Morris gets here."

While we waited for Detective Morris, Mia called the kitchen on the intercom and requested coffee be brought into the den with several cups as well as a plate of snacks for guests. I remained at the window and watched for the arrival of the police. We didn't have to wait long. I saw the gate start to open, then a dark colored sedan came on up the drive toward the front of the house. The car stopped in front of the house and two men in suits walked up to the door. I hadn't seen Koato leave the room, but he was on the front porch to greet the men. He then turned and entered the house, and the two men followed him. I turned around just as they entered the den.

The first man to come into the den was a rather tall man in his very early forties. He appeared to be in very good shape. He carried himself with an air of confidence. He was wearing a very nice sport coat and slacks. I recognized him immediately.

"I'm Detective Morris," he said as he stuck his hand out to me. "It is good to see you again, but I don't expect you to remember me."

"On the contrary, I remember you very well. You challenged me a number of times during my class on collecting of evidence and protecting the crime scene. How are you, Morris?" I asked as I stuck my hand out to him.

"Pretty good," Morris said as he shook my hand.

"What have you got going here?" he asked as he looked around at the others in the room.

"Let's take a little walk," I suggested.

"By the way, this is Officer Martin. He's new to the Detective Division. I brought him along. I hope you don't mind."

"No problem," I said as I reached out to shake his hand.

Martin shook my hand then just stood there. He was listening to what we had to say. I led Martin and Morris to the staircase and started up the stairs.

"At the moment, all I have is most likely a case of fraud, insurance fraud to be more accurate."

"You want to fill me in?" Morris asked.

As we climbed the stairs to the fourth floor, I explained what we had and how it laid out. He was a little concerned about jurisdiction since the fraud had been committed in Massachusetts. He seemed a little more interested when I explained the antique furniture that was supposed to have been destroyed in the fire was in the house. I explained I had proof that it was here.

"I don't think you will have a jurisdiction problem because the evidence is here, the person who we believe committed the crime is in New York, and the insurance company is also in New York," I said.

When we got to the fourth floor, we stepped into the first room. It was a large room that ran about halfway along the back side of the house. There was a lot of antique furniture neatly placed in long rows with spaces between the rows wide enough to move pieces of furniture between the rows without bumping into other pieces.

We hadn't gone very far down one of the rows when Monica stepped out from between two large armiores. Martin was the first to see her.

"Hey, who are you?" he asked.

"That is my wife and partner. Gentlemen, this is Monica McCord. She is an expert on antiques. She is looking for the furniture that was claimed to have been destroyed in the fire. She is checking each item against the list of items that were supposed to be in the fire."

"Good morning, gentlemen," Monica said. "Nick, I have found thirteen pieces that are on the list, so far."

"How many pieces are on the list?" Morris asked.

"There are thirty-one," Monica responded.

"Who does all this belong to?" Morris asked.

"Neil J. Cox," I said.

"Where is he now?"

"We don't know," I said. "What I do know is he filed a claim for this furniture with the insurance company. And for your information, he is one of our suspects in the disappearance of William J. Cox."

"So you were not really looking into a fraud case. You were another PI looking into the disappearance of William Cox."

"That is correct. We stumbled onto the fraud case while looking for William."

"You said he is one of your suspects. I take it you have others?"

"At least one other at this time, James MacPherson. We also think he is involved in the fraud case, but we are not sure what his involvement might be."

"What can I do to help you?" Morris said.

"We currently have William's girlfriend in a hospital in Massachusetts. We found her with James at both the MacPherson's lodge near Athol, Massachusetts, and then later at the Cox's lodge near Windsor. He had apparently been keeping her hidden from everyone for at least the past four years. She is pretty well dependent on him and scared of almost everyone.

"Let's go down to the den. I have all my evidence there. You can look over any of it you want, but we will give you a rundown on what we have to save you some time."

"Good," he replied.

The three of us returned to the den, leaving Monica to finish. When we arrived at the den, we found Koato and Mia were gone. I was glad to see that they had left. I didn't think it was a good idea for Mia to hear everything over again.

We all sat down while I continued to tell Morris everything we knew about the activities of James, Susan and William for the past five years. When I was finished, Morris just sat there. I could tell he was thinking very hard.

"So what you're saying is all this is connected to William's disappearance."

"Yes. We believe it is, but what we really want to know is what happened to William."

"Do you think he is still alive?" Martin asked.

I had thought of that myself, but somehow it sounded different when someone else said it. I had no proof either way, but I had to admit there was a strong possibility he had been killed almost four years ago. I looked at Martin, then back at Morris.

"I think there is a very strong possibility that he is dead. Even Susan, his girlfriend, hasn't seen him for the better part of four years."

"What's next?" Morris asked.

"I would like to talk to James MacPherson without his lawyers."

"That might be hard to do. All he has to do is ask for a lawyer and we have to stop questioning him."

"That is true, for you. I don't have to stop questioning him."

"That may be true, but anything you find out will not hold up in court if he claims you were an agent for the police."

I knew what he was saying was true. The real problem was how do I get him to talk to me. I had to have some leverage if I was going to get anything of value out of him. What I really needed to do was scare the hell out of him.

"I'm thinking if I were to catch him somewhere out of your jurisdiction, I might be able to get him to talk."

"Where does he work?"

"He works for an insurance company in New York City. He was the claims representative for the insurance company that had the coverage on the lodge and its contents when it burned down. He handled the claim," I explained.

"I would think that is a conflict of interest since he has a close relationship with the Coxes," Morris said.

"There is little doubt about that. I think he is the claims representative for the insurance company in at least the northern part of Massachusetts. I think that is how he was able to keep Susan Small in hiding."

"He spends a lot of time in that area?" Morris asked.

"Yes. He did."

"So what are your plans?"

"I was thinking I would go into New York City and talk to his boss. He might tell me a little about what James does and how much authority he has in doing it. If I'm real lucky, I might get a chance to talk to James again."

"If that doesn't work?"

"I guess I have to have another talk with Susan Small."

"Okay. I can put a hold on all the furniture that was supposed to have been destroyed in the fire. That will prevent Neil from taking any evidence. With the evidence you have, I should be able to arrest Neil for fraud and hold him for the Massachusetts DA, if I can't charge him for it here."

"I would appreciate that," I said as I stood up and reached out a hand.

"I'll have officers watching the gates. If Neil shows up, we'll arrest him."

"That would be good. You also might tell your officers to watch for James MacPherson. Before, he has hidden at his mother's home next door. He might be there now. You might pick him up as an accomplice. We think he helped Neil commit the crime by signing off on the claim for the furniture. He may also be in it even deeper than that," I said.

"You think he might be involved in William's disappearance?"

"He could be, but right now I think he is an accomplice in the fraud. Signing off on the claim sure supports that."

Martin stood up and waited while I shook Morris's hand, then shook his. I walked them to the door. Once they were in the car, I saw Morris make a call on his radio. I could only assume that he was setting up a surveillance of the gates to pick up Neil.

As soon as they were gone, I went looking for Mia. I found her with Koato in the garden waiting for me. I explained what arrangements were made with the local police. I told her the police were going to wait outside her property in the hope Neil would show up. I also told her that they were going to arrest him. She seemed to agree with what the police were going to do. I then went looking for Monica.

CHAPTER TWENTY-TWO

When I got to the fourth floor, I didn't see Monica. The fourth floor was more like a large attic with a high ceiling and several partitions that divided up the attic into smaller areas. As I started walking down the aisle in the center of the attic, I noticed the furniture was arranged in such a way that every piece could be easily seen without having to move something out of the way.

When I was about halfway down the aisle, I saw Monica step out from a row of dressers. She saw me and smiled as she started walking toward me.

"I take it you have found more of the furniture on the list." I said.

"I haven't finished looking, but I have found twenty-seven pieces out of thirty-one so far."

"How long do you think it will take you to find the rest?" I asked.

"Oh - maybe another half hour at the most. He didn't even try to hide them."

"He probably didn't think he needed to with them here in his house. When you're done, would you meet me in the den, please? I'll wait for you there."

"Okay," Monica said.

I gave Monica a kiss, then left her to her work. There was no sense in me staying there. I would just be in the way. She would be able to spot what she was looking for quicker, and would probably get done faster without me around.

It didn't take me long to get back to the den. I had no more then entered the room when the phone began to ring. I walked over to the phone and sat down as I picked up the receiver.

"Hello?"

"Is this Nick McCord?"

"Yes."

"Nick, Hank, the State Trooper from Massachusetts."

"Hi, Hank. What's up?"

"I just talked to the doctor. He thinks Susan Small is ready to talk about what happened to her over the past few years."

"That's great. Has she talked to you?"

"Yeah, but she talks more freely to the woman officer I had with me when you were here. She has been spending a lot of time with Ms. Small everyday and got her to open up," Hank explained.

"That's great."

"I talked to my boss. He's given me permission to bring Ms. Small down there so you can talk to her, if you think it will help your case."

"You know, it just might be the right thing to do. If we have her here, she would get a chance to talk to Mia, William's mother. I'm sure she could shed some light on what might have happened to William."

"I'll be bringing her down tomorrow with Alicia Hoffman. Can you arrange a place for us to stay?"

"I'm sure Mrs. Cox would be glad to put you up here at her home. She has plenty of room."

"That will work. I'll see you tomorrow around noon."

"See you tomorrow," I said.

Just as I was hanging up the phone, I looked up and saw Monica come into the room. She had a big grin on her face.

"I take it you found almost all the furniture from the lodge," I said.

"Better than that. I found all of it. Every piece on the list is on the fourth floor. The one I found on the third floor was not one of them, but there is one just about like it on the fourth floor."

"Great. If we have nothing else, we have Neil as the prime suspect in a very large fraud case."

"What's next?"

"Hank is bringing Susan down here to talk to us. They should be here tomorrow about noon."

"Is she talking?" Monica asked as if she couldn't believe it.

"Yes. Alicia got her to talk."

"Good. I have some news for you. James just arrived back at his mother's house. I saw him from a window on the fourth floor. He drove in and parked his car behind the house and went inside."

"Great. I've been wanting to talk to him."

I reached over and picked up the phone. I placed a call to the MacPherson's. It was answered by James.

"Hello?"

"I don't think it would be wise for you to hang up on me," I said.

"What do you want?"

"We are going to have a talk. I expect you to come over here to the Cox Estate within the next five minutes, or I will have every cop in the New England area looking for you."

"I don't think you can do that," he said, but not very convincingly.

"All I have to do is tell them you were a co-conspirator in a fraudulent insurance claim for hundreds of thousands of dollars of antique furniture, and that you were probably the one who started the fire."

"You can't prove that?"

"Let me put it to you in another way. Susan Small is ready to tell the authorities everything she knows about the fire at the lodge, the fraudulent insurance claim and your involvement in William's disappearance. Are you ready for that?"

"She won't talk to you?"

"Wrong again. She has already talked to the police. This is your chance to set the record straight. Oh, by the way. I will be visiting with your boss in New York City if you are not here in five minutes," I said, then hung up before he could respond.

Monica looked at me as if I was crazy. I had a pretty good idea what she was thinking.

"Do you think that will work?"

"I don't know, but it was all I could think of to get him out of his house. As long as he is in the house, I can't get at him."

"I hope it works," was all Monica had to say.

I returned to the window and looked out hoping that James would be coming to the gate. I was actually a little surprised when I saw James's car pull up to the gate. I was almost sure that he would run. I made a quick call to the gate to confirm it was James. When the guard said it was, I told him to let James pass, but no one else.

I hung up and watched as James drove to the front of the house. He stopped in front, but just sat in his car. I think I had a pretty good idea of what he was thinking. After a couple of minutes, he got out of the car. I left the den and went to the front door. He looked up at me when he saw me standing in the doorway.

"It was a smart decision to come and talk to me."

"It won't do you any good. I'm not telling you anything without my lawyer," he said, but his comment lacked a tone of confidence.

"You told me a lot by just coming here."

The look on his face was that of a person who was very surprised, but confused. He had no idea what he had done.

"Come inside. We are going to have a chat."

I waited for him to walk by me and enter the house. I directed him to the den.

"Have a seat," I said then watched him as he sat down on a chair.

"First of all, Susan will be here tomorrow. She is being brought here by a Massachusetts State Trooper. She was discharged from the hospital into the care of the trooper and his female partner."

I noticed the expression on his face change from that of curiosity to what could only be described as fear. To have her talk to me or any authority seemed to scare him half to death.

"I was hired by Neil Cox to find out what happened to William, but you know that. In my investigation, I have uncovered a fraudulent insurance claim filed by Mr. Cox. It was a claim he could not have filed without help, your help. Isn't that right?"

James just sat there and looked at me as if his world was starting to fall apart, which it was. The only real questions I had were what did it have to do with William's disappearance and what role did he play in it.

"Well?"

"I've got nothing to say," James said as he looked at me.

"Does your company know you and William were friends, and that you grew up living right next door to Neil Cox, who by the way, will be arrested very soon for fraud."

Again, James didn't answer, but his body language told me all I needed to know. Every nerve in his body had gone tense. He was scared.

"It is not going to be hard to prove you were involved in the conspiracy to defraud the insurance company. It wouldn't be much of a stretch to figure out that in order to keep your secrets one or the other of you killed William. The way I see it, once Neil is arrested, he will talk to save his own hide."

"He won't talk," James said.

"Well, now we're getting somewhere," I said.

"When it comes to the police, it's usually the one who talks first who gets the lighter sentence," I said, then looked at Monica.

"Would you be so kind as to ask Detective Morris to return here?"

"I'm not going to talk to him without my lawyer," James said.

"Oh, I don't care if you talk to him or not. Either way, you are going to end up in jail, probably for a very long time. How long depends on which one of you talks first."

James watched Monica as she picked up the phone. It didn't take but a few minutes before I could hear her talking to Detective Morris.

"I'll talk to you," James blurted out.

"I think it would be a good idea if you bring a tape recorder with you," Monica said before she hung up.

"Start from the beginning."

"Neil and I worked out a way to get some money by filing a fraudulent claim for the loss of the lodge and antique furniture."

"Why did Neil need money?"

"He was in debt to some guy who found out he had been selling antiques that were fakes. The guy was blackmailing Neil. He was afraid if it got out, his reputation would be ruined."

"Who set the lodge on fire?"

"I don't know. Neil hired some guy in New York City to burn the lodge. I never saw the guy. All I did was help remove the furniture two days before the fire, and help Neil file the claim."

"You did more then that," I said. "Didn't you approve the claim?"

"Yes. The insurance company didn't know that I knew Neil personally."

"What did William have to do with all of it?"

"Nothing. I don't know how William found out, but he found out his father had burned down the lodge for the insurance. That all happened at about the same time he discovered Neil was not his real father. He couldn't handle it after all the years of looking up to Neil, and believing that he was his father. He started drinking and gambling. I guess it was his way of trying to deal with it."

"Susan asked him to go talk to his father and ask Neil to do the right thing. Didn't she?" I asked.

"That's right. He went to his father, well Neil. He was hoping to get his father to go to the police to confess and take his punishment. Neil refused and they got into an argument. Neil slapped William and called him a bastard child. William threatened to go to the police."

"How is it you know all that?"

"I was with William, but I waited outside. I saw most of it through the window."

"But he didn't go to the police. Did he?"

"No. He went to his parents' cabin next to the lodge with Susan to think about what he should do. William spent the next few months trying to figure out what he should do. One day he took off to confront Neil again, but he never returned to Susan. I continued to look after her."

"You're leaving something out, aren't you?"

"What do you mean?"

"William's car was here. You took him back to your parents' cabin, not to the cabin next to the lodge. How did he get back here to confront his father?"

James almost gasped. It was the one thing he had not thought of. Even in his mind he knew there was only one way that William could have gotten from his parents' cabin to the estate, and that was if someone drove him.

"You drove him here."

There was dead silence. James was looking at his feet. It was easy to see that he was trying to think of a logical answer, but he knew there wasn't one.

"Yes. I drove him back here," he finally admitted.

"Do you know what happened to him once he got here?"

"No," James said, but there was something in his manner that told me otherwise.

"Any idea what might have happened to him?"

"Not really. The only thing I can think of was that he went to see Neil. Neil got mad and killed William."

"What makes you think that?"

"Mr. Cox would do anything to protect his reputation."

There was little doubt his last statement was true. It was at that moment Detective Morris came into the room. He was followed by Koato.

"I think Mr. MacPherson has a statement he would like to make." I said.

"We have someone else in our jail who has already made a statement." Morris said as he looked at James. "Mr. MacPherson, you are under arrest for the murder of William J. Cox."

At the moment, James almost gasped for air as his eyes grew big with the shock of the news. It was obvious that James had never considered he would be arrested for murder.

I listened while Morris read James his rights. I also watched the look on James's face while Morris cuffed him.

"Mr. Koato, I will have a forensic team out here as soon as possible. We will want to take a serious look at the old carriage house. We believe that William is buried in there," Morris said.

I could see tears form in Koato's eyes. It had to be hard on him to know his son might still be on the grounds. I walked over to Koato and reached out a hand to him. He looked up at me with sad eyes.

"Mia and I knew he was probably dead, and we tried to prepare ourselves for this time. I guess nothing ever prepares a person for the death of a child."

"I guess not. Would you like me to tell Mia?"

"No. It is best if it comes from me."

I just nodded as he turned and walked out of the room. It looked like our search for William was over. It was now up to the police to sort out the details. It came to mind that some secrets can get a person killed.

As soon as Koato left the room, I walked over to Morris. I wanted a couple of questions answered.

"Morris, I take it Neil told you what happened."

"Yeah. Neil and William went out to the barn to talk so no one would hear them. It got to be a rather heated discussion and Neil struck William. Only this time it was different. William struck back and knocked Neil on his ass. James was in the barn listening to what was going on. He was behind William. When William struck Neil, James picked up a shovel and struck William on the back of his head killing him.

"They got scared, pushed William's car out of the way, dug a hole and buried him in the carriage house, then parked the car over him. That was how the car got the dented front fender."

Detective Morris turned around and walked over to James. He took hold of one arm then walked toward the front door leading James with his hands cuffed behind him. The look on James's face showed he had given up. His life was over as he had known it. Morris stopped and looked at me.

"Thanks for all the help," Morris said. "Once we have William's body, we should be able to finish this up."

"You're welcome, but let us know if you need us."

"Could you stop by and give a statement before you return home? I never know what the defense counsel will do, but it might save you a trip back here."

"Sure. No problem," I said then watched them lead James out of the house.

The rest of the day we sort of stayed out of the way. The forensic team came out and went over the carriage house. They discovered William's body buried under the Jaguar in the carriage house.

That evening Monica and I had a quiet dinner in the dining room. Mia and Koato didn't have dinner with us. I was sure they were not all that hungry. We turned in early.

* * * *

In the morning, we joined Koato and Mia in the sunroom for a light breakfast. It was a fairly somber time. Yet, Mia seemed to want to talk about William.

"He was really a good boy. He was smart, rather sensitive. He always tried to please Neil, but nothing he did could ever get Neil to really like him. Neil pretty much acknowledged his existence but that was about it."

"I'm sure it was hard on all of you to live with such secrets," Monica said.

"Yes, it was. It was especially hard for Koato who wanted so much to be a father to William. He did his best under the circumstances," Mia said as she reached over and put her hand over Koato's hand.

"I didn't tell you yesterday because things seemed to happen so fast, but Susan Small will be arriving here this afternoon. If you don't want to see her, I will understand and have her taken back to her home in Connecticut," I said.

"No. No, we would like to meet her," Mia said. "William must have loved her a great deal to want her to be with him."

"I'm sure he did," Monica said.

After breakfast, Monica and I left Mia and Koato alone. We knew that they had a lot to think about and a lot to do. It would be a few days before they could properly bury their son.

A few minutes before noon, Trooper Hank, Alicia Hoffman, and Susan Small arrived at the estate. The meeting with Mia and Koato went very well. After a lot of tears, we all sat down to lunch. Monica and I tried to stay out of the conversation. This was a time for Mia and Koato to get to know Susan, and for Susan to get to know them.

* * * *

The next morning we joined the rest for breakfast. After breakfast, Hank and Alicia left for Massachusetts, leaving Susan with Mia and Koato. Mia wanted Susan to stay with them.

We said our goodbyes to Mia, Koato and Susan, then left for the police station. It didn't take very long for us to complete our statements and sign them. We then headed for the airport for our flight back to Wisconsin.

Once in the airport, we had a wait for our flight. Monica was watching the news on a television in the waiting area. The news was about the murder of William Cox. I didn't have much interest in it.

I looked over at Monica, then reached out and put my hand over hers. She turned and looked at me, then smiled.

"I think the first thing we should do when we get home is to find out if I'm pregnant. What do you think?"

"I think that would be a good idea," I said as I leaned over and kissed her.

The next thing I heard was the announcement that our flight was ready to board. We got up and walked to the gate, hand in hand.

Once we were in the air, we had some time to relax, the first in a long time. I had time to think about becoming a father. With what we had just gone through, there was little doubt in my mind I would make a good father. With that thought, I leaned back and dozed off.

Made in the USA
Monee, IL
19 March 2023